DYLAN THOMAS

ADVENTURES
IN THE
SKIN TRADE

An Adaptation for the Stage by

ANDREW
SINCLAIR

With a Note on the London Production by
JAMES ROOSE-EVANS

A NEW DIRECTIONS BOOK

Manufactured in the United States of America
First U.S. Edition, 1968
New Directions Books are published for James Laughlin
by New Directions Publishing Corporation,
333 Sixth Avenue, New York 10014

88478

ADVENTURES IN THE SKIN TRADE

CAST

In SAM BENNET's kaleidoscopic view of London, people play several different roles, so that the same faces reappear in different situations and characters.

MRS BENNET	MRS DACEY
PEGGY BENNET	POLLY DACEY, Salvation Army singer, Gayspot dancer
MR BENNET	MR ALLINGHAM
SAM BENNET	
RON BISHOP	Train passenger, Gayspot dancer, surrealist
ROSE	
GEORGE RING	Train passenger
LUCILLE HARRIS	
COCOABOY	Train passenger
SALVADOR	Guard, Salvation Army drummer, Gayspot dancer
FAT WOMAN	Salvation Army singer, Gayspot barmaid
TICKET COLLECTOR	Salvation Army singer, policeman
NELLIE	
SERVER	Gayspot pianist, surrealist audience
CHIPPIE	Gayspot dancer, surrealist audience
OLD TRAMP	Reporter in Gayspot, surrealist audience

SETS

PART ONE—1933

   I. *Wrath*—The Bennet house, Mortimer Street, Swansea.

  II. *Greed*—The buffet at Paddington station.

 III. *Covetousness*—Mr Allingham's house, Sewell Street, Paddington.

 IV. *Lechery*—The Gayspot night-club, Soho.

PART TWO—1936

   V. *Sloth*—The Gayspot.

 VI. *Envy*—The Surrealist Exhibition.

VII. *Pride*—Mr Allingham's.

ACT ONE

I. Wrath

The lights go up on the Bennets' living-room in Stanley's Grove, Mortimer Street, Cardiff. It is late evening. The room is the epitome of suburbia, the zenith of the provincial Welsh middle class. All the objects in the close, stuffy, claustrophobic room are three or four times life size, so that they seem to menace the people in the room with their huge immobility. Beyond the cutaway back wall of the living-room, the backdrop suggests row after row of similar suburban houses, cheek by jowl, vile villa by viler villa, stretching by a grey park surrounded by railings down to a grey, guttered sea. Throughout the play, the sets should be expressionist, representing Sam's vision of places rather than their reality, representing the essence of rooms rather than their actuality. The sets should merge, the one into the other, to give the impression of a walking dream or nightmare. The lighting should add to this effect, accentuating the world as seen in the mind of a highly emotional Welsh youth.

The Bennets' living-room contains a chintz-covered sofa, protected by antimacassars. A table and chairs, with frills on their legs to keep them from catching cold. A desk, ornate but used, and covered with schoolboys' exercise books and examination papers. An open grate with a doused fire upon it. A clock between hollow, mock-ebony, pawing horses on the mantelpiece: the time is five minutes to eleven. By the clock, a blown-up framed photograph of PEGGY BENNET *taken at her girls' school: she is all plaits and hockey-knees and black knickers. A box full of odds and ends and a cut-glass vase on the window-sill, filled with permanent flowers. Behind the vase a blown-up photograph depicting* MRS HILDA BENNET *hurrying down Chapel Street on a shopping trip: she is snapped in front of a men's clothes shop: she wears a pastelled silk scarf, a round metal badge, a cameo brooch and a knitted clover jumper. A sideboard, filled with useless and decent gee-gaws and knick-knacks, crochet-work and doilies. A mirror on the wall and a reproduction of the 'Mona Lisa'. On the ceiling, a dark circle made by the gas lights—and cracks and lines, looking like two bearded men chasing an animal over a mountain edge and a kneeling woman with faces on her knees.*

Off the living-room is a china pantry. The best plates shine in rows, a willow tree next to an ivied castle, baskets of solid flowers on top of fruits and flower-coiled texts. Tureens are piled on one shelf, on another the salad bowls, the finger-bowls, the toast racks spelling 'Porthcawl' and 'Baby', the trifle dishes, the heirloom moustache-cup. The afternoon tea service is brittle as biscuits and has gold rims.

The living creatures in the stuffy, dominating, decent room are the Bennet family: father, mother, daughter and dog—a loud, old and aunt-faced pom called Tinker, who lies snoring by the grate. MR BENNET *acts and looks like the effigy of the elementary schoolmaster: he is prim, bald and boring—he wears a starched collar and a safe suit. A pipe sticks continually out of his mouth. He carries a ruler with him, which he occasionally raps on objects, to get rid of frustrations and to practise for the knuckles of small boys. He is gentlemanly to the point of exaggeration.*

MRS HILDA BENNET *is stout, safe, confident and buried in her errands. She polishes and scrubs and scours and tidies and mothers and overbears all.*

PEGGY BENNET, *their daughter and* SAM BENNET's *sister, is tart, sharp and bright in a provincial way. She is an adept at painting blushes on her own cheeks and putting real blushes on the cheeks of others.*

Together the trio make a formidable and refined array of genteel disharmony.

4

MRS BENNET and PEGGY are clearing up the evidences of a small party, at which dominion sherry and home-made wine have been served. MR BENNET is sitting at his desk, trying to correct boys' examination papers. TINKER is snoring.

MRS BENNET. Well, that Mrs Rosser . . .

PEGGY. Saying to Mrs Baxter . . .

MRS BENNET. My husband's such a travelling man, I don't notice him missing.

PEGGY. And Mr Baxter passed over only two years back. Shall I throw away the parsnip dregs? (*Holds up half-empty wine-glass.*)

MRS BENNET. Waste not, want not.

PEGGY. (*Pouring the wine back in the bottle.*) They'll never know it's been tasted.

MR BENNET. (*Chuckling.*) You've put it in the sherry.

MRS BENNET. No one will notice.

PEGGY. Gives it body.

MRS BENNET. Don't be vulgar. (*Continues to tidy.*) It was such a nice funeral. That was when I got my black hat with the fruit on it.

Mr Bennet profits by his family's inattention to sip away at his glass of parsnip wine.

PEGGY. And the sparrow thought you were an orchard . . .

MRS BENNET. Dropped a bomb on me . . .

PEGGY. And bust his beak on a glass cherry.

MRS BENNET. It wasn't funny.

MR BENNET. (*Reading out one of his papers.*) Listen to this pearl from Jenkins minor. At the battle of Bosworth, 1066, Henry the Seventh found the crown on a gooseberry bush and said. . . .

PEGGY. (*Ironically.*) There's fascinating!

MRS BENNET. Finish 'em tomorrow.

PEGGY. If they don't finish you first.

MRS BENNET. (*Seeing her husband still drinking.*) And stop imbibing. The party's over.

PEGGY. Four glasses of parsnip wine and he thinks he's Lloyd George Almighty.

MR BENNET. I only said, at the bottle of Basworth. . . .

Tinker snores loudly.

MRS BENNET. Go and put Tinker out.

PEGGY. And put out your pipe.

Mr Bennet gets up resignedly, and obeys the various commands.

MR BENNET. There, Tinker, there's a good boy.

Tinker barks. Mr Bennet raps him with his ruler and lugs him out.

MRS BENNET. Wipe your shoes.

PEGGY. And wipe your nose.

MRS BENNET. Button your coat.

PEGGY. And button your lip.

MRS BENNET. Shut the door.

Mr Bennet opens his mouth in protest.

PEGGY. And shut up.

Mr Bennet goes out with the protesting dog, courteously bowing it first through the door.

MR BENNET. (*To himself.*) It's night outside. He could do better.

MRS BENNET. (*Shocked.*) What do you mean?

MR BENNET. (*Darkly.*) There's an alternative.

He goes out, quietly closing the door behind him.

MRS BENNET. And as for my son, Sam . . .

PEGGY. Too high and mighty to turn up at his own farewell party. There's abominable!

MRS BENNET. He's a little angel, really. Just a trifle moody.

PEGGY. Calls himself a poet. I'd call it impertinence.

MRS BENNET. You be nice about your brother. It's not everyone who's off to London in the morning.

PEGGY. Good riddance.

MRS BENNET. You'll miss the little darling.

PEGGY. Like my appendix.

MRS BENNET. Such a little treasure. Curly-haired, round-cheeked, good as gold. It seems only yesterday his face was smiling in the cradle and I went, larrikins, llareggub, lickadee! (*Makes mother-to-baby movements.*)

PEGGY. Oh, Mother!

They have finished tidying the room. Mrs Bennet brings in an empty suitcase, and puts it on the table.

MRS BENNET. We'd better get his things for London. Such a wicked city. I do hope he'll manage.

Mr Bennet enters with Tinker. He shakes his trouser leg slowly and ruefully up and down.

MR BENNET. He thought I was a lamp-post.

PEGGY. Well, if you will stand still and dream, then . . .

MRS BENNET. Lucky he didn't think you were a cutlet.

MR BENNET. Aren't I? (*Lights his pipe again.*) Lord, what foolishness.

PEGGY. Smoke, smoke, smoke. It's no fun living with a chimney in trousers.

MR BENNET. (*Ignoring her.*) Have you put in the sponge-bag, Hilda?

MRS BENNET. (*Going off-stage.*) As though I'd stop Sam from washing!

MR BENNET. All right, all right. I just asked.

MRS BENNET. (*Shouting.*) Where's his new hairbrush?

MR BENNET. That's right, shout my head off. Here it is. (*Finds the hairbrush in a drawer.*) How can I give it to you if you're in the kitchen? It's the brush with the initials—S.B.

MRS BENNET. (*Appearing with a pile of vests.*) I know his initials.

PEGGY. Mother, does he want all those vests? You know he never uses them.

MRS BENNET. It's January, Peggy. (*Her voice rises.*)

MR BENNET. She knows it's January, Hilda. You haven't got to tell the neighbours. Can you smell something burning?

PEGGY. Perhaps you left your thumb in your pipe.

Mr Bennet looks at his two hands seriously, holds up his two thumbs, shakes his head and puts his hands down. Peggy laughs.

MR BENNET. No.

PEGGY. What do you think Sam'll do first when he gets to London?

The two women continue to pack useless and careful
objects in the suitcase, until it threatens to overflow.

MRS BENNET. He'll get himself a nice room, of course, not too central. And not have an Irish landlady, you don't know how they're dirty. He'll go and get himself settled straight away. That's the important matter.

PEGGY. I'll tell him to look under the wallpaper for bugs.

MRS BENNET. That's enough of that, Peggy. Sam knows a clean place when he sees one.

MR BENNET. He wouldn't go in one, in case he made it dirty. Where is he?

PEGGY. On the slagheaps by the factory, imitating Shakespeare.

Tinker snores derisively.

MRS BENNET. He's such a shy, sweet angel, he couldn't bear the thought of company, all to do him honour. (*She brings in Sam's sensible brown town suit; and a white starched shirt with a woollen tie and a tiepin.*)

MR BENNET. I hope he remembers to call on Mrs Chapman. Give her all our love from 42, and say the roof leaks.

MRS BENNET. I'll put his wallet in his inner pocket. Not in his handkerchief one. You never know when he'll be wanting to blow his nose.

PEGGY. And scatter bank-notes to the poor and undeserving.

MRS BENNET. Oh, his Holy Bible. It does make him so cheerful, reading Ezekiel.

PEGGY. (*Bringing in a greaseproof-paper-wrapped package.*) And his sandwiches, fish paste for him specially.

MR BENNET. Won't they be stale by morning? I am.

PEGGY. Sam eats everything, so long as there's lots of it.

MRS BENNET. Help me with the lock.

They all strain and struggle to close the suitcase.

I do hope Sam's editor of *The Times* by Christmas.

MR BENNET. May take a few years longer. Rungs of the ladder first.

MRS BENNET. I'd like to be able to tell the neighbours.

PEGGY. That Sam's got a job as office boy extraordinary, for ever and always?

MRS BENNET. What a cheeky sister! (*Closing the suitcase at last.*) There. Sam's such a good boy, he's bound to be successful. I hope not too successful, or he won't come back to home and mother. (*Puts Sam's brand-new brown overcoat and hard brown hat by the suitcase, along with his black, shining shoes.*)

MR BENNET. Don't worry. The great Caradoc Evans said the Cardies always go back to Wales to die when they've rooked the cockneys and made a packet.

MRS BENNET. There's comfort.

MR BENNET. He'll make history, not teach it. The pay's better.

PEGGY. He'll get a footnote on page 700 of a critical work which sold all of eighteen copies. Sam Bennet, Welsh bard deceased, had a genius for decorating gentlemen's toilets.

> *The lights dim. In the dark the voices of the three Bennets say good night to each other in a descending scale. Tinker snores regularly as a knell.*
>
> *Enter* SAM BENNET. *He resembles Dylan Thomas's self-description. He is about five feet six inches; thick blubber lips; a snub nose; curly mouse-brown hair; one front tooth broken; speaks rather fancy; truculent; plausible; a bit of a show-off; a bombastic adolescent provincial Bohemian with a thick-knotted artist's tie and a cricket shirt dyed bottle-green; a gabbing, ambitious, mock-tough, pretentious young man. This is his façade in his known world of Cardiff. However, he can act meek as a child, when faced with the unknown. He can play up to his baby's face. In London, Sam Bennet attracts adventures to him by his own unadventurous stillness and natural acceptance of every situation. He accepts life in every position, like a baby who has been given self-dependence. He lets life come to him. Odd, very odd people come and bring him life. Whoever*

9

comes, whatever situation comes, he goes on. Then, at a
certain point, he realizes that he has shed a skin and
learnt a sin. Eventually he is stripped to his naked soul
by experience.

At first Sam peers uneasily into the known, flickering
corners of the room as though he fears that the family
might be sitting there in silence in the dark. Then he
lights the gaslight from the candle. He stands still and
listens to the noises of the house. There is nothing to fear.
He plucks up courage, and stamps lightly on the floor.

MRS BENNET'S VOICE. (*Dreaming.*) The floor's clean as a
preacher. You'll have to walk on the ceiling.

Sam leaps with fright on to a chair. Then he shakes his
head at his own weakness. He begins to lose his fear that
the strangers upstairs he has known since he can remember
will wake and come down with pokers and candles.

He puts on his brown jacket, looking good as gold and
angelic. Then he picks up the huge photograph of his
mother and looks at it reverently. Slowly he tears it into
little pieces.

SAM. Goodbye, Mother, walking down the street step by step,
stout, safe, confident, buried in your errands.

Sam destroys the framed photograph of his sister by the
clock.

Down you go, Peggy, with all the long legs and the Young
Liberals' dances, and the boys you brought home for supper on
Sunday evenings. People were downstairs all over the world.

Sam smudges his father's examination papers with coal
and tears them up and throws them about the room.

History is lies. Take old Bennet and whip him down the corri-
dors, stuff his mouth with dates. Spin him on his tellurion till his
tail drops off.

Sam begins breaking up all the more breakable objects
in the room. He unsuccessfully tries to pull the furniture
apart.

Come and look at Samuel Bennet destroying his parents' house
in Mortimer Street, off Stanley's Grove; he will never be

allowed to come back. Everyone is mad and bad in his box in Mortimer Street when the blinds are pulled. Come and see me break the china without any noise so that I can never come back. (*Makes a violent man's gesture, then is again a coward.*) Hush, I know.

> *Sam goes into the pantry and breaks a piece of china, very quietly.*

Mrs Mayor's Chain, Madame Cocked Hat, Lady Settee, I am breaking tureens in the cupboard under the stairs. (*Sam drops and smashes a tureen cover loudly and cowers like a small boy.*) Tinker did it. (*Silence. No one stirs.*) What are you doing? Leave the street alone. Let it sleep. (*Closes the pantry door.*) Ranting away? Quick now. (*Destroys in a frenzy all the remaining small objects he can find; those which he cannot destroy he stuffs up the chimney.*) These are such small things. I should break the windows and stuff the cushions with the glass. (*Sees his reflection in the mirror under the 'Mona Lisa'.*) But you won't. You're afraid of the noise. (*Turns back to his reflection.*) It ain't that. You're afraid she'll cut her hands. (*Begins to burn the edge of his mother's sunshade at the gas-mantle. He cries and tastes the tears on his tongue.*) It's salt. It's very salt. Just like in my poems.

> *Sam hangs the burnt sunshade on the 'Mona Lisa'. He puts on his hat and coat and picks up his suitcase. He is still crying. He puts down his suitcase to pat Tinker on the head. The dog gives an appreciative snore. Sam walks front stage.*

London! Where the good Cardies go to lose their seven skins on the seven sins sharp as penknives. (*Takes off his hat.*) Good morning, madam. Have you a cheap room? (*Imitating voice of an Irish girl.*) Cheaper than sunlight to you, Danny Boy. (*Normal voice.*) Has it got bugs? (*Irish voice.*) All over the walls, praise be to God. (*Normal voice.*) I'll take it. (*Laughs and waves.*) Goodbye, Mortimer Street. Goodbye, Stanley's Grove.

> *Upstairs there is the sound of movement.*

MRS BENNET'S VOICE. Sam, my angel?

> *Sam flees, terrified, as the voices of a massive Welsh choir thunder out 'Sam of Cardiff, on to Glory', . . . to the tune of 'Men of Harlech'.*

A cut-out representing the corridor of a train is pushed on by four passengers, also a train lavatory, basin and lavatory door. Sam goes and sits, fully clothed, on the lavatory. He puts his hat in the basin. The standing passengers sway and rock rhythmically to the noise of the train. Train noises sound, whistles, jolts, jerks, wheels on rails. There is evidence of steam.

A fat woman enters. She mimes squeezing past the four passengers with great difficulty: the corridor is full as an egg. The four unwillingly make way for her.

FAT WOMAN. Sorry . . . sorry . . . beg your pardon . . . excuse me . . . I am sorry . . . pardon . . . oops . . . made it.

She half pushes open the lavatory door. Sam pushes it shut again with his foot and locks it.

I beg your pardon.

She squeezes back down the line of furious passengers.

Please excuse me . . . sorry . . . I do apologize . . . pardon me . . . sorry . . . could you please make way . . . thank you.

As she squeezes past the last passenger, he pinches her. She gives a great leap and glares behind her. He bunches his hands up the arms of his overcoat, pretending that he has no hands, and smiles at her. She rolls off-stage suspiciously.

Sam is engaged in tearing up his address book and putting it in the lavatory.

SAM. Goodbye, Mrs Chapman, who is going to introduce me to a man on a newspaper. Goodbye family friends, names that might help. Ta-ta, all except Lucille Harris, the man on the pier told me of.

Sam places the page with her address on it reverently in his wallet, and imitates another man's deep voice:

Lucille Harris. She's okay. She's a girl I know. She's the best in the world; she'll take care of you. Give her a call when you're up. Tell her you're Austin's friend.

Sam pulls the chain of the lavatory, which roars and flushes.

I've eight pounds ten, a poem and Lucille Harris. Many people have begun worse. I am ignorant, lazy, dishonest and sentimental; I have the pull over nobody.

The fat woman enters again, and rudely squeezes and elbows her way past the standing and rocking four. She reaches the lavatory door, tries the handle furiously, glares.

SAM. (*To audience.*) I bet you're dancing.

The fat woman does, indeed, jig with impatience. Livid with rage, she elbows her way back past the other passengers, who are also losing their tempers. Half way along the line she collides with the ticket collector, who is coming up the line. They gesticulate and argue. The fat woman takes the collector along with her up the furious line. They begin rattling on the lavatory door.

TICKET COLLECTOR. You there. You've been there for hours.

SAM. (*To audience.*) I'm the director of the company.

The fat woman and the ticket collector elbow their way back down the line of passengers. Sam switches the water on in the toilet basin, forgetting that his hat is in the basin. He takes his greaseproof packet of sandwiches and holds it out of the window—the slipstream whisks the packet off-stage. He turns off the water, picks up his hat and, unnoticing, deluges himself with water when he puts the hat on. He walks out of the lavatory. The other passengers are all looking in the wrong direction. Sam stands to one side of the lavatory. The fat woman, the ticket collector and the guard all return, pushing past the furious standing line. There is the sound of the train slowing. The guard hammers on the door.

TICKET COLLECTOR. Ever since Neath.

The fat woman, the ticket collector, the guard and all the

passengers rush on the door and hammer away loudly.
They fight each other to get at the door. No one thinks to
try the handle.

A woman pushes on a large sign marked Paddington.
Sam gets off the train completely unnoticed.

II. GREED

The scene is an old-style British railway buffet, where all
bad food goes stale before it dies. There is a bored
CHIPPIE *and a bored* SERVER *behind the counter,*
with its tea urn, old-fashioned advertisements and glass
cases of last year's sausage rolls and rock buns. About the
room there are chairs and tables on their last legs. A
large clock tells the time for those with trains to catch or
miss. Occasional train, barrow and tea urn noises
sound.

At one table sits MR ALLINGHAM, *who has played*
Mr Bennet in the first scene. He is a middle-aged man
with a chocolate-brown birthmark over his cheek and
chin like the half of a beard. The rest of his face is red
and purple, faintly shabby and unshaven, shiftily angry
about the eyes as though his cunning were an irritation
impossible to bear. His hair is the colour of ferrets and
thin on the crown: it stops growing at the temples but
comes out again from the ears. His hat has made a deep
white wrinkle on his forehead. He wears a long scarf
round his neck and a long shabby overcoat. He has a
book propped against an empty bottle in front of him, but
he spends most of the time reading the palms of his hands,
which are covered with calculations in ink.

RON BISHOP, *a slick, smooth, greased card from*
Cardiff, from the crescent next to Stanley's Grove,
stands at the counter talking to the chippie. The creases on
his trousers are as sharp as knives.

An OLD TRAMP *with a gramophone and horn on a
pram plays scratchy thirties records on one side.*

*There is no one else as yet in the buffet. Sam walks in,
wide-eyed and wet-hatted. Throughout the scene he
guzzles his drink and gobbles his food and smacks his
lips happily.*

SAM. (*To chippie.*) Nip of Bass, please, and a ham sandwich.
RON. Hallo, Sam. Fancy seeing you up here.
SAM. Hallo, Ron. Fancy seeing you.
RON. Been up in the Smoke for long, Sam?
SAM. Just arrived. How's tricks?
RON. Same as me; we must have been on the same train. Oh,
so so. Still at the old game, Sam?
SAM. Yeah, up on a bit of business. You at the usual?
RON. Yeah. (*Silence.*)
SAM. Where are you staying, Ron?
RON. Usual. Strand Palace.
SAM. Dare say I'll be seeing you then.
RON. I dare say. (*Silence.*) Well, be seeing you.
SAM. Be good.
RON. And if you can't be good, be careless.
SAM. I couldn't.
RON. What?
SAM. Care less.

*Ron laughs and turns away from this fellow recruit from
Cardiff.*

*Sam takes his Bass and his sandwich, and goes to sit down
next to Mr Allingham. An unknown woman in a fur coat,
who later turns out to be Lucille Harris, comes in and sits
at a table away from Sam. She has a cup of coffee in her
hand. She reveals her legs up to her knees. Sam stares at
her fiercely and intently, while she tries to ignore him,
first by looking down at her lap, then by going to the
counter to buy a second cup of coffee, then by tapping her
spoon on the side of her cup, then opening and closing the
clasp of her handbag, then by turning her head round
slowly to face Sam and then by looking away again
quickly through the window.*

Sam stares continually at Lucille. She is a handsome girl of uncertain background and age, coarsely beautiful, classless and classy, an easylie easy-lay. All freeze as Sam delivers his monologue to the audience.

SAM. This is the beginning of an advance. Now she is pretending not to notice her knees are uncovered. There's a lynx in the room, lady. Button your overcoat. (*Pretending to be writing a letter with his finger on the back of an envelope.*) I'd better write a letter home. Everybody writes a letter home. Dear mother, this is to tell you that I arrived safely and that I am drinking in the buffet with a tart. I will tell you later if she is Irish. She is about twenty-eight years old and her husband left her above five years ago because of her carryings on. Her child is in a home, and she visits him every other Sunday. She always tells him that she is working in a hat shop. You need not worry that she will take all my money as we liked each other on first sight. Her business is very hard on stockings, so I am going to pay the first week's rent. And you need not worry that I shall break my heart trying to reform her, because I have always been brought up to believe that Mortimer Street is what is right, and I would not wish that on anybody.

Sam tears up his envelope, tilts his hard, wet hat over one eye and winks: a long, deliberate wink that screws up his face and makes his burning cigarette nearly touch the blunt end of his nose. Lucille snaps her handbag, pushes two pennies under the saucer and walks right out of the room, never looking at Sam as she passes.

SAM. My God, she was blushing.
MR ALLINGHAM. Did you speak?
SAM. I think I said it was a fine day.
MR ALLINGHAM. Stranger in town?
SAM. Yes, I've just come up.
MR ALLINGHAM. (*Not caring at all.*) How do you like it?
SAM. I haven't been outside the station yet.
MR ALLINGHAM. There's plenty to see, if that's what you want. Museums, art galleries. (*Silence.*) Musea. (*Shakes his head.*) There's one at South Kensington, and there's the British Museum, and there's one at Whitehall with guns. I've seen them all. You must move out of the station some time, you know. If

you want to see around. It's only fair. It's not fair to come up in a train and sit in the buffet and then go back and say you've seen London, is it?

SAM. I'm going out now, quite soon.

MR ALLINGHAM. That's right, give London a chance. Otherwise, it's like not getting out of bed, isn't it? You've got to walk round, you know, you've got to move some time. (*In a sudden, dull passion.*) Everybody does it.

SAM. (*Going over to the counter.*) Another Bass, please, miss. This is the last one, then I'm going.

MR ALLINGHAM. (*Angrily.*) Do you think I care how many more you have? You can stay here all day—why should I mind? (*Looks at the palms of his hands.*) Am I my brother's keeper? (*Silence.*) I hate a nosy parker.

> *Mr Allingham gets up and walks over to Ron Bishop and the Server at the counter. As he passes Lucille's table he takes the two pennies which she left under her plate.*

SAM. (*To audience.*) Stop thief!

> *As Mr Allingham does not stop Sam gets up, walks over and puts sixpence under the plate just as the Chippie comes over to the table.*

SAM. It fell on the floor.

CHIPPIE. Oh yeah?

> *Sam sits down, his cheeks burning. The other four nod and whisper in his direction.*

SAM. (*To audience.*) I wish I could go back home.

CHIPPIE. His type steal pennies from the blind.

SERVER. Take 'em in the middle of Piccadilly Circus and laugh when they are run over.

MR ALLINGHAM. You saw that lady in a fur coat who walked out so suddenly. He showed her a dirty postcard.

RON. Never! Where did he get it?

> *The other three look at Ron suspiciously.*

CHIPPIE. Ain't he a *friend* of yours?

RON. Never seen him in my life.

SERVER. You was talking to him, man.

RON. He was trying to cadge a meal. Rotten little beggar. 'Bye all. Time flies. Me too.

SAM. (*Calling.*) Be seeing you, Ron.

Ron exits; his face is flushed with the embarrassment of not noticing Sam. Sam smiles at the Server and he stares away at once as guiltily as though he had been discovered robbing the till.

SAM. (*To audience.*) I am not at all like that. You can count the straws in my hair.

Mr Allingham rejoins Sam at his table.

MR ALLINGHAM. I thought you were going. You told me you were going. You've been here an hour now.

SAM. I saw you.

MR ALLINGHAM. I know you saw me. You must have seen me, mustn't you, because you were looking at me. Not that I want the twopence, I've got a house full of furniture. Three rooms full to the ceiling. I've got enough chairs for everyone in Paddington to have a sit down. Twopence is twopence.

SAM. But it was twopence to the waitress too.

MR ALLINGHAM. She's got sixpence now, hasn't she? She's made fourpence clear. It doesn't do any harm to you just because she thinks you were trying to nip it off her.

SAM. It was my sixpence.

MR ALLINGHAM. (*Raising his hands in protest.*) And they talk about equality. Does it matter whose sixpence it was? It might have been mine or anybody's. There was talk of calling the manageress, but I put my foot down there. (*Silence.*) Made up your mind where you're going when you move out of here? Because move you must, some time, you know.

SAM. I don't know where I'm going. I haven't any idea in the world. That's why I came up to London.

MR ALLINGHAM. (*Restraining himself.*) Look here, there's sense in everything. There's bound to be. Otherwise we wouldn't be able to carry on, would we? Everybody knows where he's going, especially if he's come by train. Otherwise he wouldn't move from where he took the train from. That's elementary.

SAM. People run away.

18

MR ALLINGHAM. Have you run away?

SAM. No.

MR ALLINGHAM. (*In a trembling voice.*) Then don't say it. Don't say it. (*Looks at his palms, and speaks gently.*) Let's get the first thing straight. People who have come must go. People must know where they're going, otherwise the world could not be conducted on a sane basis. The streets would be full of people just wandering about, wouldn't they? Wandering about and having useless arguments with people who know where they're going. My name is Allingham, I live in Sewell Street off Praed ditto, and I'm a furniture dealer. That's simple, isn't it? There's no need to complicate things if you keep your head and know who you are.

SAM. I'm Samuel Bennet. I don't live anywhere at all. I don't do any work, either.

MR ALLINGHAM. Where are you going to go then? I'm not a nosy parker; I told you my business.

SAM. I don't know.

MR ALLINGHAM. He doesn't know. Don't think you're any-where now, mind. You can't call this place anywhere, can you? It's breathing space.

SAM. I've been wondering what was going to happen. That's what I've been discussing with myself. I came up really to see what would happen to me. I don't want to make anything happen myself.

MR ALLINGHAM. He was discussing it with himself. With a boy of twenty. How old are you?

SAM. (*To audience.*) He won't believe it. (*To Mr Allingham.*) Twenty.

MR ALLINGHAM. That's right. Discussing a question like that with a boy just out of his teens. What did you expect to happen?

SAM. I don't know. Perhaps people would come up and talk to me at the beginning. Women.

MR ALLINGHAM. Why should they talk to you? Why should I talk to you? You're not going anywhere. You're not doing anything. You don't exist.

SAM. Anyone might come up. (*Hopelessly.*) Anyone.

MR ALLINGHAM. Oh, anyone of course. Greta Garbo, Marlene Dietrich, Mae West!

SAM. You don't understand. I don't expect that kind of person. I don't know what I do expect at all, but it isn't that.

MR ALLINGHAM. Modest.

SAM. No, I'm not modest either. I don't believe in modesty. It's just that here I am and I don't know where to go. I don't want to know where to go.

Mr Allingham pleads, leaning across the table, pulling softly at Sam's collar, showing the sums on his hands.

MR ALLINGHAM. Don't say you don't want to know where to go. Please. There's a good boy. We must take things easy, mustn't we? We mustn't complicate things. Take one simple question. Now don't rush it. Take your own time. (*Menaces Sam with a teaspoon.*) Where will you be tonight?

SAM. I don't know. I'll be somewhere else, but it won't be anywhere I've chosen because I'm not going to choose anything.

MR ALLINGHAM. (*Whispering.*) What do you want, Samuel?

SAM. I don't know. (*Touches his wallet in his breast pocket.*) I know I want to find Lucille Harris.

MR ALLINGHAM. Who's Lucille Harris? (*Silence.*) He doesn't know. Oh, he doesn't know!

Sam puts the forefinger of his right and writing hand in the neck of his empty bottle of Bass.

SAM. But you don't understand, Mr Allingham.

MR ALLINGHAM. (*Loudly.*) I understand enough. You do want to make things happen, don't you? I'll make them happen all right. You can't come in here and talk to me like you've been talking. Lucille Harris. Lucy da monk! Come on. We're going. (*Scrapes back his chair.*)

SAM. Where to?

MR ALLINGHAM. Never you mind. It's I making things happen, isn't it?

SAM. I can't get my finger out of the bottle.

MR ALLINGHAM. (*Taking Sam's suitcase.*) What's a little bottle? Bring it with you.

CHIPPIE. He steals bottles too, does he? Greediguts.

MR ALLINGHAM. We paid for it.

20

CHIPPIE. (*Snatching the spoon from Mr Allingham's hand.*) And spoons!

SERVER. Lucky there aren't any babies lying around.

MR ALLINGHAM. Come on, son. (*They walk forward.*)

CHIPPIE. Father and son too.

Mr Allingham steals a chair as he leaves the buffet and conceals it under his coat.

Sam desperately tries to hide the bottle on his finger in his pocket, but he cannot.

INTERLUDE 2

The cut-out is pushed on in reverse to show a street of dirty terrace houses in the streets about Paddington. Sam and Mr Allingham seem to perambulate about with aimless purpose, never going anywhere but somehow arriving. The bottle weighs heavily on Sam's finger, but he cannot get it off.

There is the sound of hooting, brakes and traffic jams.

SAM. Where now?

MR ALLINGHAM. You follow me. And put your hand in your pocket. It looks silly.

Sam obeys and puts his hand in his coat pocket.

I've never been with anybody with a bottle on his finger before. Nobody else has ever had a bottle on his finger. What'd you want to put your finger in the bottle for?

SAM. I just pushed it in. I'll be able to get it off with soap; there's no need to make a fuss.

MR ALLINGHAM. Nobody else has ever had to get a bottle off with soap, that's all I'm saying.

SAM. Do you think I want it on? I might want to write, and whoever wrote with the end of a bottle?

MR ALLINGHAM. This is Sewell Street.

SAM. Dull, isn't it?

A Salvation Army band marches round and round the stage, the drummer threatening to knock Sam over with the swing of his drumsticks. Mr Allingham takes off his hat politely, but Sam is disgusted.

S.A. BAND. (*Sing.*)

> I'M H-A-P-P-Y, I'M H-A-P-P-Y,
> I know I am, I'm sure I am,
> I'm H-A-P-P-Y . . .

> Roll out the lifeline, roll out the lifeline,
> Someone is drifting away,
> Roll out the lifeline, roll out the lifeline,
> Someone is sinking today . . .

> Oh, when the roll is called up yonder,
> Oh, when the roll is called up yonder,
> Oh, when the roll is called up yonder,
>   (*Marching off.*)
> I'll be there!

SAM. It's just like the streets at home.

III. COVETOUSNESS

Every inch of Mr Allingham's room at Sewell Street is covered with furniture. Chairs stand on couches that lie on tables: mirrors nearly the height of the door are propped, back to back, against the walls, reflecting and making endless the hills of desks and chairs with their legs in the air, sideboards, dressing-tables, chests of drawers, more mirrors, empty bookcases, wash-basins, clothes cupboards. There is a double bed, carefully made, with the ends of the sheets turned back, lying on top of a dining-table, on top of another table: there are electric lamps and lampshades, trays and vases, lavatory bowls and basins, heaped in the armchairs that stand on cupboards and tables and beds, touching the ceiling. The one window, looking out on the road, can just be seen through the curved legs of sideboards on their backs. The walls behind the standing mirrors are thick with pictures and picture frames.

A naked white statue labelled 'Adonis' is prominent, also the old tramp's pram with the gramophone and horn.

By climbing on a pile of spring mattresses across the higgledy-piggledy of assorted furniture, a bath can be reached on an upper level of the room. Under the bath is a primitive open boiler, ready to light: the bath is full of greasy water, though there are no pipes attached to it. A carpet is laid out flat and wide beyond the bath, having no visible support. It bears a great earthenware jar dangerously upon the backs of its patterned birds. Above, a rocking-chair balances on a card table, and the table's thin legs rest on the top of a cupboard standing up straight among pillars and fenders, with its mirrored door wide open. The bath is distinct and isolated from the rest of the room: two covered bird cages hang over it.

This is the fullest room in England. Hundreds of houses have been spilt in here, tables and chairs coming in on a wooden flood, chests and cupboards soaring on ropes through the window and settling down like birds. The room is even fuller than those at Stanley's Grove. All the furniture of Sam's home and the buffet is swallowed up in this sea of flotsam.

Mr Allingham appears, climbing over the stack of mattresses. He puts the stolen chair with other stolen chairs and tables from the buffet.

MR ALLINGHAM. Hop in, boy.

Sam appears from behind a high kitchen dresser hung with carpets. He hops obediently.

It's a pity we can't cook here. There's plenty of stoves too. That's a meat safe. (*Points.*) Just under the bedroom suite.

SAM. Have you got a piano?

MR ALLINGHAM. There used to be one. I think it's in the other room. She put a carpet over it. Can you play?

23

SAM. I can vamp. You can tell what tunes I'm doing easily. Is the other room like this?

MR ALLINGHAM. Two more rooms, but I think the piano's locked. (*Distastefully*.) Yes, there's plenty of furniture. Whenever I say 'That's enough now'—in she comes with her 'Plenty more room, plenty more room'. She'll find she can't get in one day, that's what'll happen. Or she can't get out: I don't know which would be the worst. It gets you sometimes, you know, all this furniture.

SAM. Is she your wife, Mr Allingham?

MR ALLINGHAM. She'll find there's a limit to everything. You get to feel kind of trapped.

SAM. Do you sleep here?

MR ALLINGHAM. Up there. It's nearly twelve foot high. I've measured. I can touch the ceiling when I wake up.

SAM. I like this room. I think it's perhaps the best room I've ever seen.

MR ALLINGHAM. That's why I brought you. I thought you'd like it. Proper little den for a man with a bottle on his finger, isn't it? I told you, you're not like anybody else. Nobody else can bear the sight of it. Got your case safe?

SAM. It's there. In the basin.

MR ALLINGHAM. You keep your eye on it, that's all. I've lost a sofa. One more suite and I'll lose my bed. And what happens when a customer comes? I'll tell you. He takes one peek through the door and off he trots. You can only buy what's on the top at the moment.

SAM. Can you get into the other rooms?

MR ALLINGHAM. You can. She takes a dive in, head first. I've lost all interest in the other rooms, myself. You could live and die in there and nobody'd know. There's some nice Chippendale too. Up by the skylight. (*Rests his other elbow on a hall-stand*.) I get to feel lost. That's why I go down to the buffet; there's only tables and chairs there.

> Sam clambers up to sit on the edge of the bath. He swings his legs.

SAM. Aren't you frightened of things falling? Look at that rocking-chair. One little prod and over she comes.

MR ALLINGHAM. Don't you dare. Of course I'm frightened; if you open a drawer over there, a wash-stand falls down over here. You've got to be quick as a snake. There's nothing on the top you'd like to buy, is there?

SAM. I'd like a lot of things, but I haven't any money.

MR ALLINGHAM. No, no, you wouldn't have money. That's right. Other people have money.

SAM. I like the big jar. You could hide a man in that. Have you got any soap for my finger?

MR ALLINGHAM. Of course there's no soap, there's only wash-basins. You can't have a proper bath either, and there's five baths. Why do you want a jar big enough to hide a man in? Nobody I've ever met wants to hide a man in a jar, not even a man in a jam. Everybody else says that jar's too big for anything. Why do you want to find Lucille Harris, Sam?

SAM. I didn't mean I wanted to hide a man in it. I mean that you could if you wanted to. Oh, a man I know told me about Lucille, Mr Allingham. I don't know why I want to find her, but that's the only London address I kept. I put the others down the lavatory in the train. When the train was moving.

Mr Allingham squeezes the neck of the naked statue, labelled Adonis.

MR ALLINGHAM. Good, good. This is Adonis. Say hello, Adonis. (*The statue is silent.*) He's shy.

Enter ROSE, a woman with black hair and a Spanish comb in it: her face is plastered white as if it were a wall. She takes a sudden dive between two columns of chairs behind Sam and disappears. She must land on cushions or a bed, for she makes no sound.

Enter GEORGE RING, a tall, youngish man with a fixed smile: his teeth are large, like a horse's, but very white: his glistening fair hair is done in tight curls, and it smells from afar. He stands on a trampoline, bouncing up and down.

GEORGE. Come on, Rose, don't be sulky. I know where you've gone. (*Pretending to see Sam for the first time.*) Good gracious, you look like a bird up there. Is Donald hiding anywhere?

MR ALLINGHAM. I'm not hiding. I'm by Adonis. Sam
Bennet—George Ring.

> *George bows and bounces, rising a foot from the*
> *trampoline.*

GEORGE. I hope you've excused the room to Mr Bennet.

SAM. I don't think it needs any excusing, Mr Ring: I've never
seen such a comfortable room. I want it, want it, all of it, all for
my very own.

GEORGE. (*Bouncing higher and higher.*) Oh, but it's terrible.
It's very kind of you to say it's comfortable, but look at the
confusion. Just think of living here.

> *Sam, by mistake, clunks his bottle loudly against the*
> *side of the bath.*

You've got something on your finger. Did you know that?
Three guesses. (*Bounces on the trampoline.*) It's a bottle.

> *Mr Allingham puts a sunshade up to protect himself just*
> *as George's bouncing shakes down a carpet on top of him,*
> *which almost covers him completely.*

MR ALLINGHAM. You don't know anything yet. You don't
know anything about him. You wait. What are you bouncing for,
George? People don't go bouncing about like a ball as soon as
they come into a room.

GEORGE. (*Leaping below Sam.*) What don't I know about you?

MR ALLINGHAM. He doesn't know where he's going, for
one thing. And he's looking for a girl he doesn't know called
Lucille.

GEORGE. (*Still bouncing.*) Why are you looking for her? Did
you see her picture in the paper?

SAM. No, I don't know anything about her, but I want to see
her because she's the only person I know by name in London.

GEORGE. (*Making the V-sign with two forefingers.*) Now you
know two more, don't you? Are you sure you don't love her?

SAM. Of course I'm sure.

GEORGE. I thought she might perhaps be a sort of Holy Grail.
You know what I mean. A sort of ideal.

MR ALLINGHAM. Go on, you big pussycat. Get me out of
here.

GEORGE. Is this the first time you've come to London? I felt like that when I came up first too. Years and years ago.

Sam comes down the stairs and George bounces off the trampoline to sit beside him.

I felt there was something I must find. I can't explain it. Something just round the corner.

He puts an arm round Sam, who shoves it off with his bottle.

I searched and searched. I was so *innocent*. I felt like a sort of knight.

MR ALLINGHAM. Get me out of here. (*Struggles.*) I feel like the whole room's on top of me.

GEORGE. (*Putting on a convenient lady's hat.*) Perhaps you'll be lucky. You'll walk round the corner and there she'll be. Lucille. Lucille. Is she on the telephone?

SAM. (*Edging away from George and looking at him dubiously.*) Yes. I've got her number in my book.

GEORGE. Oh, that makes it easier, doesn't it. (*Bends to pick up an antique telephone: its lead disappears among the junk.*) Why don't you ring her up now? Faint heart never.

MR ALLINGHAM. It's not . . . (*Stops talking as George puts up a finger to his lips and skips out of sight to Sam, though not to the audience.*)

SAM. Do London telephones work in a special way?

GEORGE. Easy as swallowing oysters. Just pick up the receiver and ask the operator.

Sam picks up the receiver, refers to his piece of paper and is embarrassed. He is so confused that he tries to speak into the bottle on his finger by mistake.

SAM. Please miss, could I have Soho 0007?

George makes a sign to Mr Allingham, who echoes his voice in an old water-jug.

MR ALLINGHAM. (*In a falsetto.*) Oh, oh, oh, certainly, sir. I'll put you through.

SAM. That's funny. The voice sounded as if it was in the room.

GEORGE. It's the acoustics. Naughty, naughty acoustics, stics, stics, stics . . .

MR ALLINGHAM. London air's very *queer* on the windpipe.

George makes a purr-purr ringing noise with his tongue, then a click as if the receiver had been removed. He holds the end of the telephone lead in his hand and speaks into the horn of the old gramophone.

GEORGE. (*In a dulcet soprano.*) Hallo.

SAM. Is that Miss Lucille Harris?

GEORGE. The very same. What a coincidence!

SAM. I'm a friend of Austin's.

GEORGE. Austen Chamberlain's? I'm *out* to politicians.

Mr Allingham giggles.

SAM. No, Austin. The man I met on the promenade at Cardiff. He said you were the best in the world and you'd take care of me.

GEORGE. Did he now?

SAM. Will you?

GEORGE. Of course I will, dearie. Half past ten at the Gayspot. Toodle-ley-oo.

SAM. Right you are, miss.

George clicks his tongue and dances out under Sam again. He speaks in his normal voice and carries the gramophone horn in his hand.

GEORGE. Any luck, Mr Bennet?

SAM. We're meeting at the Gayspot. Do you know it?

MR ALLINGHAM. (*Proudly.*) I've been bounced from there seven times, and every time I bounce right back, like a blinking ball.

SAM. I didn't tell her my name. How will she know me?

Sam goes to sit on the trampoline.

GEORGE. She'll know you in a million. (*Makes cat noises with his lips, hunting among furniture.*) Come on, Rose. I know exactly where you are. She's in a pet. Psp, psp, psp, psp. I'm going to buy a hammock. I can't bear sleeping under all this furniture. And then I'll go to bed like a sailor.

MR ALLINGHAM. (*Still struggling behind the hall-stand.*) Tell Rose to come and get me out of here. I want to eat.

GEORGE. (*Looking at Sam through the old gramophone horn.*) She's sulking, Donald. She's mad about a Japanese screen now.

MR ALLINGHAM. Do you hear that, Sam? Isn't there enough privacy in this room? Anybody can do anything, nobody can see you. I want to eat. When is Mrs Dacey coming with a snack for us? Are you sleeping here tonight?

SAM. Who? Me?

MR ALLINGHAM. You can doss down in one of the other rooms, if you think you can get up again. There's enough beds for a harem.

GEORGE. (*Using the horn as a megaphone.*) Harum, scarum, be bold and bare 'em. You've got company, Rose, darling. Do come out and be introduced.

SAM. Thank you, Mr Allingham.

GEORGE. (*Speaking softly in Sam's ear through the horn.*) Didn't you really have any idea at all? About sleeping and things. I think it's awfully brave. You might have fallen in with all *kinds* of people. 'He fell among thieves.' Do you know Sir Henry Newbolt's poems?

SAM. (*Taking the horn to speak through.*) He threw his empty revolver down the slope.

GEORGE. (*Taking back horn.*) He climbed alone toward the eastern edge of the trees.

SAM. (*Taking back horn.*) All night long in a sea untroubled of hope.

SAM & GEORGE. He brooded clasping his knees.

> *George sinks to his knees, clasping Sam's knees, his face pressed against Sam's middle.*

GEORGE. Oooh, goodie goodie! (*Rising.*) It's so exciting to find someone who knows about poetry. (*Takes horn.*) 'The voices faded and the hills slept.'

SAM. (*Listening in horn, then taking it and putting it over his head like a coolie's hat.*) Ah, the voices *one by one* faded . . .

SAM & GEORGE. The voices *one by one* faded and the hills slept.

> *Sam takes the horn off his head and puts it by the trampoline, where he sits down.*

GEORGE. Isn't that beautiful? The voices faded. . . . I can read poetry for hours, can't I, Donald? I don't care what kind of poetry it is, I love it all.

> *George bounces on the trampoline and shakes Sam*

29

backwards and falls beside Sam, picking up a doctor's
stethoscope to listen to Sam's heart.

Do you know, 'Is there anybody there, said the traveller?'
Where do you put the emphasis, Mr Bennet? Can I call you
Sam? Do you say 'Is there *anybody* there?' or 'Is there anybody
there?'?

SAM. (*Avoiding the probing of George's stethoscope.*) I think I'd
put about the same emphasis on all the words.

MR ALLINGHAM. It isn't natural for a man not to be able to
see anybody when he's sitting right next to them. I'm not
grumbling, but I can't see anything, that's all. It's like not being
in the room.

GEORGE. Oh, do be quiet, Donald. Sam and I are having a
perfectly serious discussion. Of course you're in the room, don't
be morbid.

He sits beside Sam, discussing poetry as seriously as if in
a seminar.

But don't you think it tends to make the line rather flat? '*Is*
there anybody there, said the traveller?' I feel you do want a
stress somewhere. 'Is there anybody there, said the *traveller?*' I
mean, he might be a monk, or anyone. Or do you think, 'Is there
anybody there, *said* the traveller?' He might be deaf and dumb,
mightn't he? It is a problem. But it's so nice to have someone to
share it with.

Mr Allingham tries to move, but the statue falls against
his chair.

MR ALLINGHAM. Don't be so forward.

GEORGE. (*Rising to pick up Adonis.*) Adonis is me, really. I
modelled for him, all starkers. (*Dusts Adonis off and sets him up*
again.)

MR ALLINGHAM. You like to think you could. And don't
you call me morbid, George Ring. I remember once I drank
forty-nine Guinnesses straight off and I came home on the top of
a bus. There's nothing morbid about a man who can do that.
Right on the top of the bus, too, not just in the upper deck.

GEORGE. I think forty-nine Guinnesses is piggish.

MR ALLINGHAM. It was raining, and I never get truculent.

I may sing and I may have a bit of a dance, but I never get nasty.
Give me a hand, Sam.

> *Sam takes the carpet off Mr Allingham, who rises,*
> *rubbing his eyes, like a man waking.*

I told you, you get trapped.

> *George is clambering delicately about the room, looking*
> *for Rose.*

GEORGE. Oh, come on, Rosie. Just because you're an
actress you think you can stay under the furniture all the afternoon. I'll count five. Five, six, seven . . .

> *There is a huge crash of falling furniture. All crouch for*
> *cover.*

SAM. (*To audience.*) It's the roof falling in. Dear mother, I am
about to be buried in Paddington.

> *It is* MRS DACEY, *entering, She is a tall, thin,*
> *dignified woman, dressed in black almost down to the*
> *ankles, with a severe white collar. Her head is held primly*
> *as though it might spill. But when she smiles, her eyes are*
> *sharp and light : the dullness races from her mouth, leaving*
> *it cruel and happy. She wears a pair of spectacles with*
> *steel rims and a hanging chain. She carries a package of*
> *pies, a thermos of coffee and paper cups.*

MR ALLINGHAM. (*Taking her arm.*) Ah, Mrs Dacey. A
woman in a thousand.

SAM. (*To audience.*) God help the other nine hundred and
ninety-nine.

MRS DACEY. Take your trotter off my sleeve. (*Her voice is*
well spoken, clear, precise.) That's better. You're as sloppy as a
piglet looking for mother's milk.

MR ALLINGHAM. Keeping well, Mrs Dacey? This is a new
friend, Sam Bennet. Where's Polly?

> *Mrs Dacey hands out the pies and coffee.*

MRS DACEY. Up to no good. You're from the country. How
did you find Ikey Mo?

MR ALLINGHAM. (*Blushing.*) That's me.

SAM. I'm not from the country, really. I'm from Mortimer

Street, Cardiff. I met Mr Allingham in the station. I'm going to sleep in his flat tonight.

MRS DACEY. I'd sooner sleep in an ashpit. You've got a bottle on your finger.

MR ALLINGHAM. There, you see, everybody notices. Why don't you take it off, Sam? It isn't a decoration, it isn't useful, it's just a bottle.

SAM. I think my finger must have swollen, Mr Allingham. The bottle's much tighter now.

MRS DACEY. Let me have a look at you again. (*Putting on her steel-rimmed spectacles.*) He's only a baby.

SAM. I'm twenty.

MRS DACEY. Ikey Mo, the baby farmer. (*Calls.*) Polly, come down here. I left her at the door; dust is bad for her sinus. Polly. Polly.

POLLY'S VOICE. What for, Ma?

MRS DACEY. Come and get a gentleman's bottle off.

GEORGE. Bottle off? It sounds like a Russian composer, doesn't it, darling? (*Reappearing among the furniture.*) What a marvellous dress; you look like a murderess. (*To Sam.*) I couldn't get Rose to move. She's going to lie there for ever in a tantrum. Do tell me what's happening, everybody.

MR ALLINGHAM. It's that bottle again. Why didn't he put his finger in a glass or something? I don't know what he was poking his finger about for in the first place. It's an enigma to me.

GEORGE. Everything's an enigma to you. You can't understand the slightest touch of originality. I think it must be awful not to have any imagination. It's like a sense of humour. When it's missing, it really is. Like the link.

MR ALLINGHAM. I'm just saying not to be able to go in and buy a bottle of Bass without having to leave with the bottle on your finger seems to me like a kind of nightmare.

> There is the sound of POLLY scrambling closer. She appears beside Sam. She has a long pale face and glasses: her hair is dark and dull.

MRS DACEY. Go and help to pull his bottle off.

POLLY. (*Pulling at the bottle.*) Does it hurt? I've never done it before.

Sam falls on to his knees on the floor, writhing in agony,
as Polly wrenches unsuccessfully at the bottle.

MR ALLINGHAM. I hope you won't ever have to do it again.
I don't care if I haven't got any imagination. I'm glad I'm like I
am without anything on my finger.

GEORGE. I'm not.

Sam looks down the neck of Polly's dress as she bends
forwards. She notices, raises her head and stares into his
eyes.

POLLY. I can't get it off.

MRS DACEY. Take him up to the bath then and put some soap
on it. And mind it's only on his bottle.

GEORGE. The water in the bath's a year old, and you can't
take out the plug.

MR ALLINGHAM. But it's very good for the duck.

POLLY. Come on, Sam.

GEORGE. Scream if you want me, I'll be up in a wink. She's
the most terrible person, aren't you, darling? You wouldn't
catch little Georgie going up there all alone.

Polly pulls Sam by the bottle on his finger up to the
bath, perched high among the furniture.

MR ALLINGHAM. (*Looking at his pie bitterly.*) I'm not com-
plaining. I'm just making a statement. I'm not saying it isn't all
as it should be. He's got a bottle on his finger. (*Picks his nose.*)
And I've got a nose on mine.

The lights dim on the rest of the room and pick out the
bath, walled off by carpets and what-nots from the
remaining space. Polly takes the covers off the bird cages.
The birds begin to sing. Sam sits on the bath's edge.

POLLY. It's only the birds. You needn't be frightened.

SAM. It's a funny place to have birds.

POLLY. They're mine. Mr Allingham says they sneer at him
and blow little raspberries all the time he's washing. But I don't
think he washes very much. Don't shout for George Ring to
come in. He's queer. He puts scent all over his underclothes;
did you know that? The Passing Cloud, that's what we call him.
The Passing Cloud.

SAM. I might be the sort that would make you want to scream.

POLLY. (*Gravely.*) I don't care. My name's Mary, but they call me Polly for short.

SAM. It isn't much shorter, is it?

POLLY. No, it's exactly the same length.

Polly sits by Sam on the edge of the bath.

SAM. Will you take off your glasses, Polly?

POLLY. If you like. But I won't be able to see very far.

SAM. You don't have to see very far, do you? It's only a small room. Can you see me?

POLLY. Of course I can. You're right next to me. Do you like me better now?

She takes off her glasses and stores them in her bosom, watched by Sam.

SAM. You're very pretty, I suppose, Polly.

POLLY. (*Unsmiling.*) Pretty Polly. (*Takes his finger with the bottle on and pulls it on to her lap.*) Nothing ever happens in Sewell Street.

SAM. (*Wincing with pain as Polly pulls the bottle.*) Nothing ever happens where I come from, either. I think things must be happening everywhere except where one is. All kinds of things happen to other people. So they say, and I want them to happen to me.

POLLY. (*Drawing her hand across her throat.*) The man who was lodging next door but one cut his throat like this before breakfast.

SAM. (*To audience.*) On my first free day since I was born, I'm sitting with a loose girl in a locked bathroom, by a dirty bath with my hand where it didn't ought to be, only with a bottle on of course. O Lord, make me feel something, make me feel as I ought to, here is something happening and I'm cool and dull as a man in a bus. Make me remember all the stories. I caught her in my arms, my heart beat against hers, her body was trembling, her mouth opened like a flower . . .

POLLY. Listen to the old birds.

SAM. (*To audience.*) I must be impotent. (*To Polly.*) Why did

34

the man next door cut his throat like that, Polly? Was it love? I think if I was crossed in love I'd drink brandy and whisky and crème de menthe and that stuff that's made with eggs.

POLLY. It wasn't love with Mr Shaw. I don't know why he did it. Mrs Bentley said there was blood everywhere, everywhere, and all over the clock. (*Rises to feel the bath water.*) He left a little note in the letter rack and all it said was that he'd been meaning to do it ever since October. Look, the water'll drip through right into the kitchen.

SAM. Perhaps it was love, really. Perhaps he loved you, Polly, but he wouldn't say so. From a distance.

POLLY. Go on, he had a limp. Old Dot and Carry. How old are you?

SAM. Twenty.

POLLY. No, you're not.

SAM. Well, nearly.

POLLY. No, you're not.

Silence. Polly flicks water on to Sam's face and moves around the bath.

SAM. Pale hands I love.

POLLY. Beside the Shalimar. Do you, Sam? Do you love my hands?

Polly spreads her menacing hands all over Sam's face, then she stalks him slowly round the bath as he edges away.

That's a funny thing to say.

Polly sits beside Sam on his other side on the bath and stares in front of her.

It's like evening here.

SAM. It's like evening in the country. Birds singing and water. We're sitting on a bank by the river now.

POLLY. (*Sadly.*) Having a picnic. Flies. *Horse* flies.

SAM. And then we're going to take our clothes off and have a swim. Gee, it'll be cold. You'll be able to feel all the fish swimming between your legs.

POLLY. I can hear the 47 bus too. People are going home to tea. It's cold without any clothes on, isn't it? Feel my arm, it's

35

like snow, only not so white. Grey, really. (*Sings.*) Pale hands I love. Do you love me altogether?

SAM. I don't know. I don't think I feel anything like that at all. I never do feel much until afterwards and then it's too late.

POLLY. Now it isn't too late. It isn't too late, Sam. We're alone. Polly and Sam. I'll come and have a swim with you if you like. In the dirty old river with the duck.

SAM. Don't you ever smile, Polly? I haven't seen you smile once.

POLLY. You've only known me for twenty minutes. I don't like smiling much, I think I look best when I'm serious, like this. (*Saddens her eyes and mouth.*) I'm a tragedienne, I'm crying because my lover's dead. (*Tears come to her eyes.*) His name was Sam and he had green eyes and yellow hair. He was ever so short. Darling, darling, darling Sam, he's dead. (*Weeps.*)

SAM. Stop crying now, Polly. Please. Stop crying. You'll hurt yourself.

> *Sam puts an arm around her shoulder, only his hand still has the bottle on, which covers Polly's face and is not very comforting.*

Nobody's dead, Polly, darling.

> *Polly cries and moans his name in the abandon of her made grief, tears at the loose low neck of her dress, throws back her hair and raises her damp eyes to the birds in their cages.*

You're doing it fine. (*Shakes her shoulders.*) I've never seen such fine crying. Stop it now, Polly, please, while you can stop. I'll do anything you like if you'll only stop. You'll drown yourself, Polly. I'll promise to do anything in the world.

POLLY. (*Drying her eyes on her bare arm.*) I wasn't really breaking my heart, silly. I was only depicting. What'll you do, then? Anything? I can depict being glad because my lover's not really dead too. The War Office made a mistake.

SAM. Anything. I want to see you being glad (*pause*)— tomorrow. You mustn't do one after the other.

POLLY. It's nothing to me, I can do them all in a row. I can do childbirth and being tight and——

SAM. You do being quiet. Do being a quiet lady sitting on a bath, Polly.

POLLY. I will if you'll come and have a swim with me. You promised. (*Pulls at Sam's bottle, torturing him.*)

SAM. Where?

POLLY. In the bath. You get in first, go on. You can't break your promise.

SAM. (*To audience.*) George, gallop upstairs now and bite your way through the door. She wants me to sit with my overcoat on and my bottle on my finger in the cold, greasy bath and there isn't room enough for two with the duck. (*To Polly.*) I've got a new suit on!

POLLY. Take it off, silly. I don't want you to go in the bath with your clothes on. Look, I'll put something over the light so you can undress in the dark. Then I'll undress too. I'll come in the bath with you. Sam, are you frightened? (*Pulls at Sam's tie, as if to throttle him.*)

SAM. I don't know. Couldn't we take our clothes off and *not* go in the bath? I mean, if we want to take them off at all. Someone might come up. It's terribly cold, Polly. Terribly cold.

POLLY. You're frightened. You're frightened to lie in the water with me. You won't be cold for long. Besides, I'll light the old boiler.

SAM. But there's no sense in it. I don't want to go in the bath. Let's sit here and you do being glad, Polly.

Polly holds the bottled finger in a vice between her legs.
Sam cannot bear the agony.

POLLY. You're frightened. I'm not any older than you are. (*Whispering.*) As soon as you get in the bath I'll jump on top of you in the dark. You can pretend I'm somebody you love if you don't like me properly. You can call me any name.

SAM. (*After a long pause, with a grin of delight.*) Lucille?

POLLY. If you like. (*Urgently.*) Give me your coat. I'll hang it over the entrance. Dark as midnight. (*Hangs Sam's coat over the entrance into the bath-hole.*) Are you undressing? I can't hear you. Quick, quick, Sam.

Sam begins to undress. He strips down to socks and pants

37

alone, having great trouble taking his jacket and shirt off over the bottle.

SAM. (*To audience.*) Take a good look in the dark, Mortimer Street, have a peek at me about to take a dip in London. I don't want to drown. (*To Polly.*) I'm cold.

POLLY. I'll make you warm, beautifully warm.

While Sam finishes stripping and gingerly lowers himself into the bath, Polly fusses about, lighting an old boiler.

As Sam sits in the water a rubber duck on a spring appears on the edge of the bath indicating the level of the rising water. Sam tries to hit the duck down with the bottle on his finger, but it bobs up persistently again.

POLLY. (*Singing.*)
> Polly, put the kettle on,
> Polly, put the kettle on,
> Polly, put the kettle on,
> And we'll all have tea . . .

I'm going to give you some brandy. I'll give you a big glass. You must drink it right down.

SAM. (*To audience.*) Come and have a look at impotent Samuel Bennet from Mortimer Street off Stanley's Grove trembling to death in a cold bath in the dark near Paddington station. I am lost in the metropolis with a rubber duck and a girl I can't see pouring brandy into a tooth-glass. The birds are going mad in the dark. (*To Polly.*) I'm in the bath now.

Polly rustles her clothes, but she does not undress. She takes a bottle and a glass from under the bath. It is eau-de-Cologne. She fills the glass.

POLLY. I'm undressing too. Can you hear me? That's my dress rustling. Now I'm taking my petticoat off. Now I'm naked. (*Holds the glass to Sam's mouth.*) Here's the brandy, Sam. Sam, my dear, drink it up and I'll climb in with you. I'll love you, Sam, I'll love you up. Drink it all up, then you can touch me.

SAM. (*Swallowing from the glass.*) Crippen! (*Louder.*) Cripes!

The lights black out, then go up to find Polly gone, and Mr Allingham, Mrs Dacey and George Ring standing

about the bath, from which only a hand with a bottle on
its finger feebly waves.

MR ALLINGHAM. Do you see what I see? He's taking a little dip.

GEORGE. Don't let me look, Donald, he's nearly bare all over. And he's ill too. Silly Sam.

MR ALLINGHAM. Lucky Sam. He's drunk, George. Well, well, well, and he hasn't even got his bottle off. Where's Polly?

MRS DACEY. You look under there. Under the bath. He's drunk all the eau-de-Cologne.

GEORGE. (*Collecting Sam's clothes and taking them down.*) He must have been thirsty. And now I can't smell nice.

George lays Sam's clothes down, puts on a cook's hat and apron and begins making Sam a prairie oyster. Mrs Dacey follows George down-stage and begins making Sam a cup of tea, while Mr Allingham helps Sam out of the bath and picks up an African shield and gives it to Sam to cover his nakedness.

MR ALLINGHAM. We mustn't épater les bourgeois.

Sam tries to step off a steep drop, but Mr Allingham prevents him and guides the staggering Sam down to the mattresses, where Sam falls, half expiring.

He's eccentric, that's all I'm saying. I'm not preaching, I'm not condemning. I'm just saying that other people get drunk in the proper places. But our Sam, no, what he wants he wants now, he simply has to get it.

MR ALLINGHAM.
MRS DACEY.   }(*Singing.*)
GEORGE.

> Picture you upon my knee,
> Tea for two and two for tea,
> Can't you see how happy we would be,
> No friends or relations
> On week-end vacations . . .

MRS DACEY. (*Forcing a cup of tea down Sam's mouth.*) Tea. Tea with plenty of sugar every five minutes. That's what I always gave Mr Dacey, and it didn't do a bit of good.

MR ALLINGHAM. Not too much Worcester, George; don't bury the egg.

SAM. Listen to the birds.

Mr Allingham, Mrs Dacey and George keep on singing as
they try to force the prairie oyster down Sam's throat.
Sam swallows it and splutters.

MR ALLINGHAM.

MRS DACEY.   } *(Singing.)*

GEORGE.

> We wouldn't let it be known, dear,
> That we own a telephone, dear,
> We would raise a family,
> A boy for you, a girl for me,
> Can't you see how happy we
>   would be . . .

GEORGE. Try some Coca-Cola, Donald. It can't do any harm;
he's had tea and a prairie oyster and everything.

MRS DACEY. *(Examining with fascinated distaste the teacup.)* I
used to pour the tea down by the pint, and up it came, lump
sugar and all.

MR ALLINGHAM. *(Failing to get Sam to drink from a Coke
bottle.)* He doesn't want a Coca-Cola. Give him a drop of your
hair oil. I know a man who used to squeeze boot-blacking through
a veil.

GEORGE. You know everybody piggish. He's trying to sit up,
the poor darling.

SAM. *(Sitting up.)* Polly's gone.

MR ALLINGHAM. You're naked too, under the testudo.

Sam grabs at the long scarf round Mr Allingham's neck
and sucks at it and bites it. Mr Allingham tries to pull
the scarf away.

No, Sam. Naughty. No. Dirty Sam. Dirty. Naughty. Mustn't.

GEORGE. Here's a nice wet sponge. *(Sponges Sam.)* Keep it on
your forehead. There, like that. That better?

MRS DACEY. *(Without disapproval.)* Eau-de-Cologne is for
outside the body. I'll give our Polly such a clip. I'll clip her on
the ear'ole every time she opens her mouth.

MR ALLINGHAM. Whisky I can understand. But eau-de-
Cologne! You put that on handkerchieves. You don't put
whisky on handkerchieves. I don't.

GEORGE. No, mustn't suck the sponge, Sam. Weaning-time. (*Pulls the sponge out of Sam's mouth.*)

MR ALLINGHAM. I suppose he thinks red biddy's like bread and milk.

> *Sam is dressed by George in his shirt, tie, trousers and jacket. He puts his clothes on with difficulty because of the bottle.*

SAM. It was the brandy from under the bath.

MR ALLINGHAM. Give me furniture polish. Especially when I'm out of sorts in the bath.

MRS DACEY. (*Calling.*) Polly! Polly!

> *There is no answer.*

GEORGE. She's depicting being glad on the landing.

MRS DACEY. Polly! (*Hunts for Polly among the furniture.*) I want to slit you.

GEORGE. (*To Sam.*) Silly goose. (*Smiles at Sam with ferocious coyness.*) You might have been drownded. (*Slyly.*) Drownded.

MR ALLINGHAM. (*Lighting a cigarette, and watching the match until it burns his fingers.*) Lucky you made a splash as you went under, I suppose. (*Puts his fingers in his mouth.*)

GEORGE. Our maid at home always said 'drownded' and 'chimbley'. You know, for chimney. I put baby on the chimbley pot and, my, didn't he smoke!

MR ALLINGHAM. Do you often get like that, Sam? The water was over your scalp.

GEORGE. And the dirt!

SAM. It wasn't *my* dirt. Someone had been in the bath before. It was cold.

MR ALLINGHAM. (*Nodding.*) Yes, yes. That alters the situation, doesn't it? Dear God, you should have gone in with all your clothes on like everybody else.

MRS DACEY. (*Reappearing.*) Polly's gone. (*Puts her hand on Sam.*)

SAM. (*Shivering at her touch.*) Oooh!

MRS DACEY. (*Mothering Sam about the hair and mouth.*) Still cold, baby?

GEORGE. (*Combing Sam's hair into place.*) You looked so defenceless, Sam. Lying there all cold and white.

> *The lights dim as evening approaches.*

GEORGE. Like one of those cherubs in the Italian painting, only with a bottle on your finger of course.

MRS DACEY. (*In her tidy, lady's voice.*) What did our Polly do to you, the little tart?

MR ALLINGHAM. I'm not listening. Don't you say a word, Sam, even if you could. No explanations. There he was, gassed in the bath at half past four in the afternoon. I can stand so much.

SAM. I want to go out.

GEORGE. I want, I want. What a tiny wanton!

MR ALLINGHAM. (*Throwing Sam an unwinding roll of toilet paper.*) Out the back?

SAM. (*Throwing the roll back.*) No, you fool. Out. London is happening everywhere. Let me out.

MR ALLINGHAM. Out then. It's six o'clock. Can you walk, Sam?

SAM. I can walk okay; it's my head.

MR ALLINGHAM. Walks on his head too.

Mrs Dacey strokes Sam's hair with the lizards that are her fingers. Sam cries out.

I've got no sympathy. Are you coming, Sue?

MRS DACEY. Depends where you're going.

GEORGE. (*Winking.*) We're going to the Gayspot. To meet Lucille.

MRS DACEY. As I'm not going to pay, who is?

GEORGE. Sam is. I looked in his wallet and he's got eight pounds inside it.

MR ALLINGHAM. He said he hadn't any money.

GEORGE. My, my, what a naughty fibber! (*Kisses the statue.*) You be good, Adonis.

MRS DACEY. Well, soon he won't have any money, will you, my little Sam?

SAM. It's for starting my future . . .

MR ALLINGHAM. You've started already, wanting things to happen. You can't say you've ended.

MRS DACEY. What you want, you pay for. Cash for what you covet . . .

SAM. I want Lucille!

They all laugh, and walk Sam, held up between them, determinedly forwards.

The cut-out of the street of dirty terrace houses is pushed on again, while the OLD TRAMP *wheels away his gramophone on the pram.*

The sound of the song 'You May Not Be An Angel' provides dance music, and the four go into an elaborate dance on their way to the Gayspot. The street sees George bouncing like a ball; Mrs Dacey, black as a deacon, jumping high over the puddles with a rustle and a creak; Mr Allingham, on the outside, stamping and dodging along the gutter; Sam gliding light and dizzy with his feet hardly touching the ground, his bottle swinging in the air, without will, as a suit of feathers, while Mrs Dacey's umbrella rides over them like a bird.

A POLICEMAN *walks on, and each stops dancing as he or she reaches the policeman. Only Sam tries to button-hole the policeman with his bottle, but George pulls him away while Mr Allingham raises his hat politely.*

As they dance off a man in a mac, chubby and hatted and smoking a pipe, pushes a small cut-out of the statue of Eros in Piccadilly Circus across the stage and off; with his free hand, he picks his nose.

MR ALLINGHAM. Piccadilly Circus. The world's umbilicus. See the man picking his nose under Eros? That's the Prime Minister.

The cut-out is wheeled off, and the four dancers find themselves in the Gayspot.

IV. LECHERY

The Gayspot, Soho. It is like a coal cellar with a bar at one end and tables and chairs: several coalmen are dancing with their sacks. There is a bright entrance above where the bath used to be: steps curve down from it to a microphone.

COCOABOY *dances with* NELLIE, *black liquorice with white junket. All the cast except Lucille are in*

the Gayspot in night-club guises, including a fat
BARMAID. *The women puss and spy about the room,*
unaware of their dancing, feeling the arms around
them as though around the bodies of different women:
their eyes are for the strangers entering, they go
through the hot movements of the dance like women
in the act of love, looking over men's shoulders with
remote and unconniving faces. The men, white and
black, are all teeth and bottom, flashers and shakers,
with little waists and wide shoulders, in double-
breasted pin-stripe and sleek, licked shoes, all ageless,
unwrinkled, waiting for the fleshpot, proud and silent
and friendly and hungry—jerking round the smoking
cellar under the centre of the world. The music *comes*
from a piano played by a pale white cross boy whose lips
are always moving.

Sam dances in with the three from Sewell Street, and
gawps at the pornographic dancing.

MR ALLINGHAM. The salt of the earth. The foul salt of the
earth. Drunk as a pig. Ever seen a pig drunk? Ever seen a
monkey dancing like a man? Look at that king of the animals. See
him? The one who's eating his lips. That one smiling. That one
having his honeymoon on her feet.

NELLIE. (*Slapping her partner, Cocoaboy.*) Find a sow to put
your trotters on.

The Sewell Street set push through the dancers towards
the bar.

MR ALLINGHAM. Three whiskies. What's yours, Sam? Nice
drop of Kiwi?

BARMAID. Kiwi's boot polish.

MRS DACEY. (*Still keeping a stranglehold on Sam's neck.*) He'll
have a whisky too. See, he's got his colour back. (*Softly.*) You're
safe with me. Once I take a fancy I never let go.

GEORGE. (*Dancing up and down at the bar.*) I'm all rhythm.
It's like a kind of current in me. It's rippling out of me,
sssssssssss . . .

SAM. Tantivvy.

44

MR ALLINGHAM. That's right. Always the right word in the right place. Tantivvy! I told you, people are all mad in the world. They don't know where they're going. They don't know why they're where they are. All they want is love and beer and sleep.

MRS DACEY. (*Squeezing Sam.*) I wouldn't say no to the first. (*To the barmaid.*) Don't pay any attention to him. He's a philosopher.

> Mrs Dacey snatches a pound note from Sam, hands it to the barmaid, then rises to dance with Cocoaboy.

BARMAID. (*Pouring out four more whiskies.*) Calling everybody nasty. There's people live in glass houses.

GEORGE. (*Looking ecstatically at the ceiling.*) People think about all kinds of other things. Music and dancing. (*Skips about.*)

MR ALLINGHAM. Sex.

GEORGE. Sex, sex, sex, it's always sex with you, Donald. You must be repressed or something.

NELLIE. (*Fiercely.*) Sex.

> All say 'sex' one after the other, in a whisper.

MRS DACEY. Sex is all right. You leave sex alone.

MR ALLINGHAM. Of course I'm repressed. I've been repressed for fifty years. I've been repressed so long I can't tell tit from tat.

BARMAID. You leave sex out of it. And religion.

GEORGE. (*Dancing and chanting.*) A *tom* tit, a *tom* tit . . .

SAM. Where's Lucille? I want Lucille.

ALL. (*Calling.*) Lucille! Lucille! Lucille! (*They laugh and catcall.*)

GEORGE. I knew she was a kind of Holy Grail. (*Whispers in the ear of one of the men.*)

> Sam puts up his hand in the air.

MRS DACEY. You may. (*All laugh.*)

SAM. Does anyone know Lucille Harris?

MAN. I'm Lucille Harris.

GEORGE. Like the tweed.

SAM. (*Horrified.*) Not *you*.

ALL. She is, she is.

MAN. I am, I am. At least, to *you.*

SECOND MAN. Betrayer! You aren't!

SAM. (*Relieved.*) I *knew* it.

MR ALLINGHAM. It's all the same in a hundred years. (*Drinks.*) They put hair oil in it. (*Gasps.*)

BARMAID. (*Flicking Mr Allingham's shoulders with her cloth.*) Keeps away the dandruff.

SAM. They speak just like the women who wear men's caps and carry fishfrails full of empties in the Jug and Bottle of the Compasses at home. Good as gold. I thought you said this was a low place like a speakeasy.

MR ALLINGHAM. Speak easy yourself. They don't like being called low down here. (*Quietly.*) They're too low for that. It's a regular little hell-hole. It's just warming up. They take their clothes off soon and do the hula hula; you'll like that.

GEORGE. Nobody knows Lucille.

SAM. It's early, I know she'll be coming. She said so.

ALL. Said so, said so, said so . . .

GEORGE. Are you sure she isn't Lucy? There's a lovely Lucy.

SAM. No, Lucille.

GEORGE. 'She dwells beside the springs of Dove.' I think I like Wordsworth better than Walter de la Mare sometimes. Do you know 'Tintern Abbey'?

MRS DACEY. Doesn't baby dance? (*Sam shakes his shoulders and her hand off his neck.*)

NELLIE. (*Dancing again with Cocoaboy.*) I got a sister in Tintern.

GEORGE. (*Pouting.*) Tintern Abbey.

NELLIE. Not in the abbey, she's a waitress.

GEORGE. We were talking about a poem.

NELLIE. She's not a bloody nun.

MR ALLINGHAM. (*Raising his fist.*) Say that again, and I'll knock you down.

COCOABOY. (*Puffing his cheeks.*) I'll blow you down.

MRS DACEY. (*Levelling her umbrella.*) Now, now.

MR ALLINGHAM. (*As the umbrella taps his waistcoat.*) People shouldn't go around insulting nuns then.

COCOABOY. I'll blow you down. I never insulted any nun. I've never spoken to a nun.

46

MRS DACEY. (*Driving her umbrella at his eyes.*) Now, now. (*He ducks.*) You blow again, I'll push it up your snout and open it.

GEORGE. (*To Sam.*) Don't you loathe violence? I've always been a terrible pacifist. One drop of blood and I feel slimy all over. Shall we dance?

Sam is taken out by George to dance. The music starts up again.

SAM. But we're two men.

GEORGE. Yeah.

SAM. Is this a fox-trot?

GEORGE. They never play fox-trots here, it's just self-expression.

SAM. What sort of a girl is Polly Dacey really? Is she mad?

GEORGE. Not so heavy, Sam. You're like a little Jumbo. When she went to school she used to post mice in the pillar-box and they ate up all the letters. And she used to do things to boys in the scullery. I can't tell you. You could hear them screaming all over the house.

As they dance Sam begins to wave his bottle about, overcome with self-expression.

Don't swing the bottle. Don't swing it. Look out! Sam! Sam!

Sam's arm flies back. He crowns Nellie. She brings down Cocoaboy, and grabs at Sam's legs.

He brings down George. Another man falls, grabbing at Nellie's skirt, which is torn off. The whole room descends into a brawling mass, a heave of bellies and arms, on the floor.

George leaps up on to the steps to have a good look at the intertwined mass and to report what's going on to Mr Allingham and Mrs Dacey.

Ooh, look. Mrs Cavanagh's ripped her skirt and she's not wearing anything underneath. My dear, it's like Ancient Rome up here.

Cocoaboy gets out of his trousers and hands them to Nellie, who is decently surrounded by the rest. Nellie puts on the trousers.

47

Now she's wearing a *man's* trousers, and he isn't. You've got legs like a spider's, all black and hairy.

BARMAID. (*Pointing to Sam.*) It was that one's fault. He crowned her with a bottle. I saw him.

> *The pile disengages itself, slowly gets upright. All form an accusing ring round Sam.*

COCOABOY. We'll get that bottle off.

> *Cocoaboy takes hold of the bottle on Sam's finger and tries to pull it off. Mr Allingham hangs on to Sam, Nellie on to Cocoaboy. Two chains form, until a tug-of-war has developed over the bottle on Sam's finger. Sam howls with pain as the tug-of-war see-saws backwards and forwards across the stage. Finally Cocoaboy lets go of the bottle, and all fall down, the bottle still on Sam's finger.*

> *There is a fanfare and* LUCILLE *appears spotlighted in the bright entrance wearing only a tiger-skin and sequins, twirling an ostrich plume. Sam gets up, a rapt unwrapped expression on his face, and makes for Lucille up the stairs. He holds out the bottle on his finger to her. There is a hush. She pulls it off easily.*

LUCILLE. There you are, ducks. What's all the fuss about?
SAM. Lucille!
LUCILLE. Lucy Laguna, if you please.
SAM. Lucille Harris.

> *All cheer this fantastic discovery.*

LUCILLE. (*looking around.*) Sssh. How do you know?

> *They come down the stairs.*

SAM. The girl in the buffet.
LUCILLE. The wee Welsh winker. (*To the pianist.*) Let's jelly-roll! (*Picks up the microphone and goes into her number.*)

> Don't ask me for more than I can give you,
> I give you what I am,
> Don't ask me to do what I can't do,
> Because I don't give a damn.

I can always find a home,
So, baby, I want you to know,
Better take me as I come,
Because I can always go.

If you don't like the rub of my skin,
You want it another way,
Well, it's the skin that I live in,
And that's how it's going to stay.

I'm a girl who likes to roam,
So, baby, I want you to know,
Better take me as I come,
Because I can always go.

I don't want none of your grumbles,
About what I do or say,
That's the way this cookie crumbles,
And that's how it's going to stay.

I'm all of what I own,
So, baby, I want you to know,
Better take me as I come,
Because I can always go.

All cheer and whistle at the end of the song.

SAM. Bloody marvellous. Another round of whiskies.

MR ALLINGHAM. Fickle Sam. I thought you wanted Lucille.

SAM. It is Lucille.

GEORGE. (*Admiring Lucille's legs, bare except for a string of sequins.*) I said she'd be here. Hallo, Lucy, what a pretty skirt!

MRS DACEY. With spots on.

MR ALLINGHAM. Of course you don't exist. So I shake you by the hand. It's quite logical, only it doesn't bear thinking of.

MRS DACEY. (*Refusing to shake Lucille's hand.*) Pleased to meet you, I'm not sure.

LUCILLE. Is this your family?

SAM. No, just people I'm staying with in London.

LUCILLE. Funny, they look just like your family.

GEORGE. Sam's my little brother, little baby Sambo.

SAM. My name's Samuel Bennet. I'm a friend of Austin's.

LUCILLE. Austin who?

SAM. Austin, from the Promenade, Cardiff.

LUCILLE. Not Austin.

SAM. Yes, Austin.

LUCILLE. Austin's an ass.

SAM. More like an asterisk.

LUCILLE. (*Laughing.*) Now we can be friends, because we've got an enemy.

GEORGE. Austin for the knackers, in his frilly knickers.

SAM. Cut off his head, and use it as a football.

LUCILLE. Mince up his liver into hundreds and thousands.

SAM. Pull down his trews, and tan him like a kipper.

LUCILLE. What do you do, Sam, pretty, curlybaby Samuel?

GEORGE. (*Sings.*) Sam is a poet, and don't we know it.

LUCILLE. Sam's a babyboy, all bib and tucker. He can't be a poet.

NELLIE. He's too young to roll a reefer . . .

BARMAID. Or drink a Bloody Mary. Pardon the language.

MRS DACEY. He should be in rompers, not in a rough-house.

MR ALLINGHAM. He's never seen a woman, except through a keyhole.

SAM. Oh yes, I have. I've made thousands.

LUCILLE. Of purls and plains for bed-socks?

SAM. Of girls and verses.

GEORGE. Read us a poem, then. I love poesy . . .

MR ALLINGHAM. Don't ask him. Or there'll be trouble with the Lord High Chambermaid. (*All shout for Sam to read a poem.*)

SAM. (*Diffidently.*) Well, there's one I sent in for a prize . . .

BARMAID. Booby prize.

NELLIE. Booby hatch.

COCOABOY. Looney bin.

ALL. Upsadaisy, Sam. Read your little poem.

> *They push Sam up on the stairs. At first haltingly and diffidently, and then convinced and meaning it, Sam declaims. The Gayspot people all pretend to listen to him seriously, but they howl with silent laughter and play tricks on him as he reads, until he has to give up because of noise and mirth.*

SAM. The force that through the green fuse drives the flower
  Drives my green age, that blasts the roots of trees
  Is my destroyer.
  And I am dumb to tell the crooked rose
  My youth is bent by the same wintry fever.
BARMAID. Do you feel crooked, Rose?
LUCILLE. He's a bent youth . . . I like that.
GEORGE. It's beautiful, Sam. Go on. Just like Ella Wheeler Wilcox.
SAM. The force that drives the water through the rocks
  Drives my red blood, that dries the mouthing streams
  Turns mine to wax.
  And I am dumb to mouth unto my veins
  How at the mountain spring the same mouth sucks.

Cocoaboy makes a loud sucking noise. All laugh.

GEORGE. Beasts. It's lovely, Sam.

Sam slaps away at the lewd hands about him and shuts up.

MR ALLINGHAM. You should have left the bottle on his finger. Stopped him writing any more of that rubbish. Don't know where we are any more. Of course he could use rhyme and metre like everybody else, but he's Sam Bennet.

Sam descends off the stairs sadly. Lucille puts an arm round him.

LUCILLE. Not to worry. I'm glad I took your bottle off. I'm sure you can use your fingers for other things.
MRS DACEY. Just like my Polly. Another little tart.
SAM. (*Shyly.*) Living's better than literature, don't you think, Lucille?
GEORGE. What about loving, little brother Sam?
LUCILLE. I'll love you, and live with you, and never, never leave you. Nobody ever wants to write in the middle of a night with me. This is the original skin they used to wrap Elinor Glyn in.
MR ALLINGHAM. That's it. Build Britain's Babies. Don't dirty up her pages.
SAM. Bye, bye, Sam Bennet, author and poet, pighead and

88478

potboiler, the good old three-adjectives-a-penny Rimbaud of Stanley's Grove, Cardiff. Up with Romeo Sam, the ladies' man . . .

LUCILLE. With a Soho, and an oh-ho . . .

SAM. For love, life, lechery, and . . .

SAM & LUCILLE. Lucky Lucille!

Sam and Lucille embrace. All clap and whistle and jeer.
The lights dim. The Gayspot people freeze. Sam looks up
into the sole spotlight and says simply :

SAM.   In my craft or sullen art
Exercised in the still night
When only the moon rages
And the lovers lie abed
With all their griefs in their arms,
I labour by singing light
Not for ambition or bread
Or the strut and trade of charms
On the ivory stages
But for the common wages
Of their most secret heart.

Not for the proud man apart
From the raging moon I write
On these spindrift pages
Nor for the towering dead
With their nightingales and psalms
But for the lovers, their arms
Round the griefs of ages,
Who pay no praise or wages
Nor heed my craft or art.

BLACK OUT

End of Act One

ACT TWO

V. Sloth

The lights go up on the Gayspot, in the early afternoon, three years later. All who were there previously are frozen into their identical positions at the end of Act One. They slowly and reluctantly move out of their set positions to group themselves about the room: they move in time to the tired musical repetition of Lucille's song from Act One, played at half-speed. The only addition to the personnel of the room is Polly Dacey, who forms with Mr Allingham and her mother exactly the same proud, suffocating, cloying group that Sam has fled from in Wales. The Sewell Street set have become the literary family of the successful minor poet, Sam Bennet: the others in the room have changed their habits and dress to those of would-be 'literati'. Only George resents Sam for taking his place in the affections of the Sewell Street set.

The bored and slothful Lucille, wearing shabby-genteel clothes, is sitting at a table beside Sam. He has a sack on his head and he is tied with a double length of rope round his arms. Every so often he gives a spasmodic twitch as though he is still trying to get out, but he has obviously been in the sack for so long that everyone is ignoring him. He has won the reputation of being an 'enfant terrible', and is always being egged on to some new folly, despite his many bourgeois traits. He only wears now a tattered shirt and cardigan and trousers under the sack.

ALL. (*Ironically.*) Lucky Lucille!

LUCILLE. It's like calling a sweep lucky.

POLLY. That's talking, when you've got the great Sam Bennet as your lusty lover.

LUCILLE. He's a bloody fiasco. All beer and no skittles. A pint pot of froth. (*Sadly.*) He brings me out in spots.

53

POLLY. Some'd like to be in your shoes.

LUCILLE. I'm size seven, duckie. (*Sings.*) Your feet's too big.

SAM. (*Muffled.*) I want out. Out.

MR ALLINGHAM. He wants out. Then why did he ever get in there? It's too much. The first time I ever saw him three years ago he had a bottle on his finger. And now he has a sack on his head.

SAM. Help me out, someone. I can't get out by myself.

GEORGE. (*Nastily.*) Listen to him now. Houdini Sambo. The Great Escapologist. Said he could get out of *anything*.

SAM. Help me out.

Polly goes over to help Sam out, but George pushes her away.

GEORGE. Not yet. There's still five minutes to go. It's a bet. He said he could get out of anywhere in forty minutes like Houdini. And he *can't*.

SAM. I'll get out.

He gives a great spasmodic heave, then collapses back, apathetic beside the apathetic Lucille.

GEORGE. You didn't think I could tie such a good granny-knot, did you? Well, I could. I learnt it from my granny.

Mrs Dacey walks up and shoves the blocking George to one side with the point of her umbrella.

MRS DACEY. Push off. Or I'll stick you.

She unties the ropes off Sam with one flick of the knot.

There you are. Easy does it. Poor baby, you shouldn't let them talk you into it. They're always egging you on. And where would you be without Momma Dacey to help you?

Mrs Dacey pulls the sack off the coughing Sam.

SAM. I want out, out of you all, out of London. Back to Wales. It's no worse.

LUCILLE. (*Shoving a beer glass across to Sam.*) Have a Bass and drown it.

As Sam begins to talk a REPORTER like a Boswell jots down every word.

SAM. Look. This is like a mouldy morgue shuttered on a Sunday. I could bring my Auntie here.

MR ALLINGHAM. And the vicar's wife. A regular little vestry.

SAM. (*Walking about the bar on the bag.*) First time I came three years ago, it was all ripe, rude and whorey-roaring. Tarts ten a penny, and I had sixpence. Eyes like scissors to lop off my buttons. London an eight-million-headed harem . . . on *heat*.

MR ALLINGHAM. Don't you believe everything you see, especially if it's after dark. This is all pretending.

SAM. It's just women with shabby faces and comedians' tongues, squatting and squabbling over their mother's ruin. They might have lurched in from Llanelly on a football night.

> *The reporter taps Sam on the shoulder at the outlandish Welsh name, so that the exasperated Sam has to repeat himself.*

Llan-eth-ly! . . . on the arms of short men with leeks.

BARMAID. No leaks in here. You leak in the proper place.

SAM. (*Looking at the barmaid with withering contempt.*) Look. Dull as sisters, red-eyed and thick in the head with colds. They sneeze when you kiss them, or hiccup and say *Manners* in the dark traps of the hotel bedrooms. (*Pause.*) Do you think the thirties will ever end? (*Pause.*) I thought not.

MR ALLINGHAM. They may end us. (*Putting the side of his head on the bar.*) I keep my ear to the ground. (*Declaiming.*) O to be in Moscow, where everybody's free, And Stalin is the Santa Claus of the Land of Liberty.

GEORGE. O to be in Berlin, I think that Hitler's fine. Who minds if he's a Nazi if the trains run on time?

> *There is laughter, then a silence.*

SAM. (*Cuttingly.*) You could almost hear a name drop.

GEORGE. Your own?

> *There is another silence.*

NELLIE. (*To Sam.*) Free booze, if you amuse me.

LUCILLE. Do something outrageous.

COCOABOY. Shatteringly shocking.

POLLY. Do you strip well, or is that your mother?

SAM. (*Pushing away the surrounding sycophants.*) I don't want to shock anyone. Leave me alone.

NELLIE. Go on, Sam, you're so clever.

GEORGE. Such a bad little bourgeois . . .

MR ALLINGHAM. The zenith of obscenity . . .

MRS DACEY. Naughty, naughty, naughty . . .

GEORGE. The Leonardo of innuendo . . .

POLLY. Emperor of smut.

SAM. (*Unwillingly.*) I wish I were a plumber. Then I could flush myself.

All laugh loudly and sycophantically.

NELLIE. Another whisky for Sam.

LUCILLE. He's a witty bit of a nit.

POLLY. A porno pet of a poet.

GEORGE. The Wordsworth of the W.C.s.

SAM. (*More happily.*) Did I tell you about when I stayed with the Armitages? They hadn't talked to each other for twenty years, so they used to leave each other messages on the toilet paper to show how they felt for each other. So when I sat down I had to use stuff like, 'Dear Tom, I hope this finds you as it leaves me. Peggy.' Or 'Dear Peggy, I wish you were here. Tom.'

They all laugh again in happy hero-worship, as they cluster about their chief and clown.

LUCILLE. Cut the cackle, and down to the verses.

POLLY. The poem that won the prize, and nobody understood.

MRS DACEY. Except us.

MR ALLINGHAM. Although it was widely circulated in all the pulp press . . .

GEORGE. To be wiped on the asses of the masses . . .

MR ALLINGHAM. In piam memoriam . . .

GEORGE. Samuel Bennet, poet laureate unappointed.

MRS DACEY. (*Proudly.*) Go on, Sam. 'The force that through the green fuse . . .'

SAM. (*Rudely.*) Blows the lights.

MRS DACEY. From your loving Momma Dacey.

POLLY. Please, for Pretty Polly, Pretty Polly.

SAM. Cuckbloodyoo to you.

LUCILLE. Go on, Sam. Your only excuse is that you're a flipping poet. Do you think I'd put up with you, bed, boredom, body and booze, if I didn't think you were something a little bit special? A dead girl's only got a future on the nib of a poet.

GEORGE. So here's for posterity!

SAM. Don't you mean posteriors?

Sam is lifted up on the bar. This time all hush themselves reverently. The coming minor poet is about to read. The scene is in complete contrast to that at the end of the first act. Now Sam half mocks his own reading and throws it away, while the others listen in rapt attention as to a cathedral preacher or a swearing navvy. The reporter takes notes. Only on the last two lines does Sam suddenly become sad and bitter with his feelings.

SAM. The force that through the green fuse drives the flower
 Drives my green age; that blasts the roots of trees
 Is my destroyer.
 And I am dumb to tell the crooked rose
 My youth is bent by the same wintry fever.

 The force that drives the water through the rocks
 Drives my red blood; that dries the mouthing streams
 Turns mine to wax.
 And I am dumb to mouth unto my veins
 How at the mountain spring the same mouth sucks.

 The hand that whirls the water in the pool
 Stirs the quicksand; that ropes the blowing wind
 Hauls my shroud sail,
 And I am dumb to tell the hanging man
 How of my clay is made the hangman's lime.

 The lips of lime leech to the fountain head;
 Love drops and gathers, but the fallen blood
 Shall calm her sores.
 And I am dumb to tell a weather's wind
 How time has ticked a heaven round the stars.
 (*Bitterly.*)
 And I am dumb to tell the lover's tomb
 How at my sheet goes the same crooked worm.

There is a roar of cheering and back-slapping in which only the jealous George Ring does not join.

NELLIE. Beer for everybody.

COCOABOY. A yard of ale for Sambo.

SAM. Make it a mile.

The barmaid sets up drinks for everybody as they mill about the bar in an admiring circle. The women particularly squash against Sam and paw him. Sam drinks hugely and steadily.

George leaps up on to his table.

GEORGE. Now you can hear *my* latest poesy. (*Declaims.*) Laugh and the world laughs with you,
Weep and you weep alone,
For the sad old earth . . .

A universal groan bursts from the Gayspot people.

SAM. (*Ironically.*) Lovely, George. Just like Ella Wheeler Wilcox.

GEORGE. (*Getting down.*) It *is* Ella Wheeler Wilcox.

Nellie begins pawing Sam in real earnest.

LUCILLE. (*To Nellie.*) Keep your paws off.

NELLIE. I was just *touching*.

MRS DACEY. He's real all right. You don't have to handle.

POLLY. (*Fondly fingering Sam.*) Symbol Simon.

Lucille slaps Polly's hand off and tries to stop Sam from drinking a whisky on top of his beer.

LUCILLE. You'll get canned.

SAM. I'm already sardined with women.

MR ALLINGHAM. We're all oiled all right.

SAM. Oiled all right. Imagine, all of us, oiled in the oilymost ends of the earth under the lubricious oilyverse . . .

GEORGE. (*Determined to join in the act somehow.*) Greasy oil over, vamping with vaseline, feeling oilright and just wonderfoil . . .

The Gayspot people begin to make train noises and whistle as a background rhythm.

SAM. When we took a train, there'd be oil on the tyres and oil on the wheels and you'd hear the porters snorting, 'Oil Change, Clapham Junction . . .'

MR ALLINGHAM. So we'd go to Rome and ask for an audience, and there's never an audience far away when our Sam's oiled and talking. And we'd say to the guard at the gates of the Vatican: 'We want to see his Oiliness,' and the Cardinal would oiler down from his window: 'Oil off till Oilmas.'

Sam hands George up to stand on the table again.

SAM. Then, when the oily and the ivy 'ang on the Oilmas tree in Trafalgar Square, we'd all greet the oily occasion with praises to the Oilmighty. (*Sings.*)

Oil things bright and beautifoil . . .

All join hands to dance round the table.

ALL. (*Singing.*)
Oil creatures great and smoil,
Oil things wise and wonderfoil,
Are made of . . . *Oil. Oil. Oil.*

Mrs Dacey puts her closed umbrella between George's legs and suddenly opens it. He seizes it and leaps to the ground, using it as a parachute.

GEORGE. Oil Hitler!

All freeze in their positions, as Sam slumps at a table to address the audience.

SAM. (*Gloomily.*) The trouble is, it's true. We're up to our eyes in a gusher, thicker than treacle. (*Sighs.*)
Oh no work of words now for three lean months in the bloody
Belly of the rich year and the big purse of my body
I bitterly take to task my poverty and craft:
To take to give is all, return what is hungrily given
Puffing the pounds of manna up through the dew to heaven,
The lovely gift of the gab bangs back on a blind shaft.

Sam goes into a horrible spasm of coughing, which ends with him spitting on the floor. He examines the result with gloomy satisfaction.

It's blood, that's the stuff.

GEORGE. You can't stop Sam from doing irritations. I mean imitations. My unfavourite imitation is One Lung Sam, the T.B. Man. Roared out from *both* bellows.

Sam gives a great cough again.

MR ALLINGHAM. Of course if you really were a lunger, you'd have a reason for getting a load on. But you can't be Keats, you know, if your output's only bar stories and your consumption's only froth.

The Gayspot people cry shame to Mr Allingham.

SAM. I'll beat Keats to the undertaker. You'll be sobbing gin into my grave-clothes. And the sooner the better. (*Drains his mug of beer.*) If there's one thing worse than an empty glass, it's a poet who can't produce. I should have stayed clotted in Cardiff...

Sam's eyes suddenly widen with horror as Ron Bishop enters again in shining new commercial traveller's clothes and bowler hat, carrying a little case full of samples. He immediately recognizes Sam. Sam goes into a fake spasm of graveyard coughing, turns his back and buries his face in his hands as Ron rushes up to remind him of the past.

RON. Did I hear Cardiff? What a coincidence. Sam Bennet, I said I'd be seeing you and I'm only three years late.

BARMAID. We're just closing, mister.

RON. That's all right, miss. I've just seen my old pal Sam from Stanley's Grove.

Sam continues coughing, turned away from Ron.

GEORGE. (*Stealing Ron's bowler.*) Is he for real or is he a sample?

LUCILLE. He's forged. (*Puts on the bowler and raps it with her knuckles.*) What did I tell you? Hollow.

POLLY. He squeaks if you press his belly-button.

MRS DACEY. Don't you dare, you doxy.

Polly approaches Ron, touches his waistcoat, screams, runs away and hides.

POLLY. I don't dare. He's vegetable.

GEORGE. Perhaps he's come to sell *himself*.

MR ALLINGHAM. But who would buy him?

GEORGE. (*Approaching very close.*) Do you think I smell of violets or orange-blossom?

Ron goes brick-red with embarrassment and comes over to Sam, who cannot avoid him.

RON. Well, how's tricks, Sam? Haven't heard a sausage from you in three years down in Cardiff except in the papers. Proper little nob now, aren't you, eh?

SAM. (*Mumbling.*) I don't think we've met.

RON. (*Eagerly.*) Oh yes, we have. I'm Ron. Ron Bishop. Socks and suspenders and ladies' haberdashery. You know my line.

He puts his suitcase of samples in front of Sam.

GEORGE. (*Pushing Ron back to the Gayspot people.*) Any friend of Sambo's a *special* friend of mind.

MRS DACEY. (*Jabbing at Ron with her umbrella.*) He's wearing a corset under his suit. He only shows it to old ladies.

POLLY. Lend us your samples, ducks. (*Snatches open Ron's suitcase, and throws foundations and underclothing all over the room.*)

LUCILLE. Woo, shocking stockings.

GEORGE. And knickers you can see through. (*Puts a pair of diaphanous pants over his head.*) I spy . . . sinfulness.

> *Ron runs about the room in pursuit of his samples. All improvise with the samples to the fury of Ron. They lead him on like bull-fighters, trout-fishers, teases. They play games with the clothes, pull them about, burn them, wet them, ruin them. They seize Ron's hat and umbrella and take them to pieces.*

RON. (*Desperate and nearly weeping.*) Hey, give 'em back. Give 'em here. Don't. I won't half cop it at the office. They're mine. Be sports, eh?

BARMAID. Stop that, you. This is a respectable bar. I won't have filthy men selling filthy things in a filthy way here. (*Clouts him with her wet dish-cloth.*)

RON. Stop 'em, Sam. You know me. Give me a hand, there's a good chap.

SAM. (*Coughing like a churchyard.*) Slap my tubercules, someone.

> *Mr Allingham slaps Sam's back with such a will that Sam nearly cracks his spine straightening. Sam immediately puts his hand to his face.*

Ow, no. It's a fly in my eye.

Mr Allingham works on the cowering Sam fiercely with his handkerchief.

BARMAID. (*Hitting Ron with her dish-cloth.*) Out with you! Out with you! Hop it!

MR ALLINGHAM. (*Working on Sam's eye.*) Out, out, vile jelly.

All yell, egging on the barmaid. Ron makes for the door, routed with his scattered samples thrown after him and at him as he speaks.

RON. (*Bitterly.*) Oh, you've come a long way, Sam Bennet, with your poetry and too-good-for-you manners and your fine friends a decent chappie wouldn't be seen dead with, but to me you're still a nasty dirty little squirt with a cut-glass accent, trying to be better than he should be, the snot-nosed snob from Stanley's Grove who swallowed a dictionary. I'll tell 'em you're too far gone to ever come back.

Ron goes out with some dignity. All the hangers-on in the Gayspot follow him.

POLLY. You didn't really know the horrible thing?

GEORGE. Of course he did. But Sam's ashamed of his old friends. I'm not, am I, Donald? I may know everybody who's anybody. But I'll still be your friend when Sam's long gone and forgotten you.

MR ALLINGHAM. Sam's loyal as a limpet. He wouldn't sell my statue behind my back. Make me flog Adonis so he could suck up to his fancy friends. Sam didn't know that Thing from the Outer Suburbs.

SAM. (*Feebly.*) Of course not. He must have mistaken me for another Sam Bennet who looks just the same.

LUCILLE. But you do come from Cardiff.

SAM. That explains the likeness. It must be my long-lost cousin, who lives next door.

MRS DACEY. (*Fondly holding Sam.*) Aren't families awful?

SAM. Why do you think I left mine?

BARMAID. Closing time, gentlemen, *if* you don't mind.

All gulp down the remainder of their drinks and make for the door. Sam is held firmly and escorted in the bosom of his adopted family. The barmaid stacks up all the bar furniture out of the way.

MRS DACEY. Where shall we go now?

SAM. They've closed time everywhere.

LUCILLE. I've got an appointment. Abyssinia. (*Goes off.*)

MR ALLINGHAM. We'll have to go and find Adonis. I know the galleries. They're like the Inquisition. They *stretch* canvases and *hang* pictures.

GEORGE. My friends the surrealists will take extra good care of Adonis. He likes being on exhibition.

MR ALLINGHAM. You keep away from me, George Ring. Go and see your new friends. (*Anguished.*) Adonis! You made me betray him, sell him to the slavers. Now Adonis is gone, my room is empty.

MRS DACEY. At least they paid for him. And we never even sniffed the money. Like putting it down a sewer, into your pocket.

POLLY. Your room's not empty without your silly statue. It's still the fullest room with a roof on. You can't complain. I couldn't believe it the other day. I found some *air* in there.

MR ALLINGHAM. Empty, empty. Every time I see that gap where my lovely Adonis was, I think, Take all the rest but leave me my Adonis.

GEORGE. You are an awful old carry-on, Donald. But I don't care now. Ever since Sam came you haven't tried to understand me. (*Hissing at Sam.*) Home-wrecker!

MRS DACEY. (*To Sam.*) He's always like that whenever he sells anything. You'd think they'd cut off his thumb.

POLLY. Why don't we?

MRS DACEY. Shut up, or I'll slit you. (*Softly to Sam.*) He can't bear to give anything up. (*Feels Sam's neck.*)

SAM. Or anyone. (*Unmoving.*) I want out.

MRS DACEY. He always hangs on. We call him the Chippendale Leech. You have to burn him off with a cigarette.

MR ALLINGHAM. Empty, empty. Where art thou, my Adonis?

GEORGE. (*Conciliating.*) Right here.

MR ALLINGHAM. Not you, you . . . ringworm.

GEORGE. (*Very hoity-toity.*) Well, no one may appreciate me here, but There Are Those Who Do, as you shall see shortly. (*Exits.*)

BARMAID. Closing time, I said.

The barmaid finishes stacking up the bar.

The lights darken on the stage as the Sewell Street set come forward.

SAM. On to bloody limbo till the lights go up and it's opening time again and the booze keeps us ticking over till another. . . .

BARMAID. Closing time. Closing time. All closed now.

The stage is in semi-darkness. The surrealists set up the next set of the exhibition.

MR ALLINGHAM. You better be careful what you've done to my Adonis, you Dalis and Dadas and damfools.

POLLY. (*Sings.*) Oh, Dada wouldn't buy me a bow-wow,

ALL. Wow-wow.

POLLY. Dada wouldn't buy one at all,
　　　 I've got a little cat
　　　 And I'm very fond of that,
　　　 But . . .

SAM. (*Sings, to the tune of Tipperary.*) Goodbye, Salvador Dali . . .

ALL. 　　Farewell, Gertrude Stein,
　　　 Of Hemingway you be wary,
　　　 Picasso's a swine.

A POLICEMAN *halts the four from Sewell Street, blows his whistle and raises his truncheon. The singing stops. He indicates the Surrealist Exhibition. As the lights go up to reveal the exhibition he turns to reveal himself a surrealist. For a patch has been cut out of the back of his uniform and on his bare shoulder-blades has been tattooed the legend—I Love Sade.*

VI. ENVY

The scene is the Surrealist Exhibition in the New Burlington Galleries in 1936. A huge mouth spans the stage from wing to wing. Four objects dominate the front of the stage. A large jug covered with fur. A stool with four real human legs. A wickerwork model with a clock face sitting in the pram. And a monster red apple by which SALVADOR *is standing, a proud man in black downturned moustaches and a black overcoat.*

On high stands a SURREALIST *in a skin-tight suit covered with symbols and bulbs. Alternately the bulbs flash on and off like a Christmas tree.*

There is a red dustcloth over a standing object in the shape of a woman. Most prominent is a round object in the shape of a woman's belly. A pair of steps leads up to a window in the middle of the object. It is entitled 'Womb with a View', but its form only suggests its subject abstractly. It is on the high level where the bath was: steps lead to it.

Weird dissonances sound.

Round the exhibition gawp the audience; the Sewell Street set also gawps, impressed, and George rushes about trying to be always on the fringe of the centre of attention and on the edge of the swim. Sam is made to feel awed by the cock-snooking, anti-bourgeois quality of the works, which make his efforts to shock seem so petty. He is both delighted by and envious of the exhibition.

The surrealist in the winking bulbs points at George as he comes forward proudly carrying a pedestal, which he sets down on the ground by Salvador.

GEORGE. Hail, Caesar.

SALVADOR. I came. (*Sits on the pedestal.*) I sat. (*Gets up and carries off pedestal.*) I departed.

 The audience claps admiringly.

SAM. Childish. Jumble-mumble and gibble-gabble.

POLLY. (*Coming up.*) You're envious.

SAM. I'm not.

POLLY. Your eyes are green like a cat's with a wish-I'd-have-done-it. Look, Sam, there's a tea-set made of fur.

SAM. To keep the tea warm? Clever.

POLLY. And a monster apple.

SAM. For a monster Eve. (*To audience.*) No temptation here.

POLLY. (*Pointing at the huge mouth.*) Oooh, that's a big kiss.
SAM. Go on then. Don't let me stop you.
POLLY. You won't. I want to be kissed all over.

> *Polly writhes about in front of the big kiss.*
> *Sam walks away from Polly. George puts a saucepan full*
> *of boiled string in his hand.*

GEORGE. Hand it round. Salvador says so.
SAM. What is it? Macaroni?
GEORGE. Boiled string.
SAM. Why's it boiled?
GEORGE. You couldn't eat *raw* string, could you?

> *Sam shrugs and begins to hand round the boiled string to*
> *all and sundry.*

SAM. (*Shouting.*) Free samples! Delicious! Keeps the guts together!
MR ALLINGHAM. I'm hungry. (*Takes some of the boiled string and eats it.*) It's boiled string.

> *He hands the mass of string back to Sam, who gets his*
> *hands entangled in it.*

SAM. Exactly. Weak or strong?
MR ALLINGHAM. Oh, Sam Bennet isn't like anybody. He eats string for breakfast, and sucks stamps instead of lollies.
SAM. Give me a hand with it.
MR ALLINGHAM. He wants a hand when he's got two already. He could do with a hand when he's got one to spare. (*Turns away.*) Adonis! (*Examines wickerwork model in the pram.*) They've starved him to death.

> *Mr Allingham decides that perhaps the model is not*
> *Adonis and begins a detailed search of all the objects. As*
> *he looks under them and takes them apart the surrealists*
> *shoo him away. But he continues in his quest, determined.*

> *The surrealist with the bulbs points downwards and winks*
> *as Salvador enters carrying a folded chair.*

SALVADOR. The ear is a chair.
SAM. No, it isn't.
SALVADOR. The ear is a chair.

SAM. Whoever sat in an ear?

Salvador opens out the chair to reveal a large ear painted upon it. He sits on the chair to a round of applause.

SALVADOR. Voilà.

As Salvador walks off with the chair he pulls the dustcloth off the standing object to reveal MISS ROSEBUSH, *a girl dressed in a long black velvet dress which leaves her shoulders bare. From the neck upwards her face is a mass of roses. On her neck is a large snail. She stands as still as a statue to a great round of applause. All gather round this new object, oohing and aahing.*

Sam fights his way through the crowd to get close. He is obviously fascinated.

MRS DACEY. Don't get too close. She's covered with snails.

SAM. (*Handing her the saucepan.*) And slugs. You sound just like my mother.

The crowd drifts away. Polly approaches. Sam is still entangled in the string on his arm.

MRS DACEY. What's she advertising?

MR ALLINGHAM. Weed killer.

POLLY. Is she real? (*Sneezes.*)

MRS DACEY. Keep off. Roses are bad for your sinus.

SAM. They aren't real roses. They're false.

Polly touches Miss Rosebush's bosom.

POLLY. So's them.

SAM. They're breathing!

POLLY. Bet you it's a bicycle pump.

SAM. She's alive. (*Prods Miss Rosebush's arm.*) My finger goes right in.

POLLY. She's a soft statue.

Sam lifts up Miss Rosebush's arm, which sticks in mid air. Sam tries to pull it down again, but it won't go. Sam hangs desperately on to the arm, but it won't go down.

SAM. It's stuck.

POLLY. There you are. The clockwork's stuck. I told you she wasn't real.

Mr Allingham comes up to prod the statue of Miss Rosebush.

MR ALLINGHAM. Is my Adonis in *that*? (*Shakes his head.*) No, he wouldn't be.

SAM. I want her. I want out with her.

MR ALLINGHAM. (*Wandering off.*) Adonis.

MRS DACEY. Don't you fall for a silly statue now. Look where it's got Ikey Mo. *Gaga.*

POLLY. Oooh, look.

They all look up to see George, half naked, appear on the steps. He strikes up a pose. Round his neck hangs the sign, Mobile Adonis—Do Touch. *The crowd paws him.*

GEORGE. Ooh, velvet paws. Velvet paws.

Mr Allingham goes up to George furiously and shoves him up the steps.

MR ALLINGHAM. You can't pretend you're an Adonis. You're a free-for-all. I don't need you. I don't need anyone. I need my Adonis. You show me where they've put him.

GEORGE. I don't know, Donald. Really I don't.

Mr Allingham pushes George along with him to help in the search for the lost Adonis.

Sam has moved away two steps from the statue to watch the scene with George. Suddenly the statue of Miss Rosebush moves two paces sideways, her arm still pointing outwards, and touches Sam on the cheek. He leaps a mile.

SAM. She moved!

POLLY. She was always there, silly.

SAM. She moved. She touched me.

POLLY. Nonsense. You backed into her.

SAM. She moved, I tell you.

POLLY. Go on.

She pulls Sam away. As he moves away with her the statue glides forwards and touches Sam again. Again he leaps.

SAM. There. She *did* touch me.

POLLY. (*Turning.*) She's on wheels.

SAM. She's on feet, can't you see? You look. I'll prove it.

He takes a step away, stops, then suddenly swings round.
The statue has not moved. He loiters along, then suddenly
whirls back. The statue still hasn't moved.

POLLY. You can't play grandmother's footsteps with a silly old statue. You'd wait for ever.

She walks forwards, turning Sam round and away. The
statue glides up and touches Sam again. This time Sam
catches her by the hand and won't let go. The string is still
wrapped round one of his arms.

SAM. Go on, of course she's real. She's got warm fingers. Aren't you, Miss Rosebush?

POLLY. They can do wonders with rubber these days.

SAM. I love you, Miss Rosebush. I do. Please speak to me. (*Pause.*)

MISS ROSEBUSH. (*In a low warm voice.*) I haven't got a voice.

POLLY. There. What did I tell you? It's a record. Hidden in her navel.

SAM. Let me see you.

MISS ROSEBUSH. I haven't got a face.

SAM. She's shy. We've got to be private.

POLLY. You can't be. It's an exhibition.

SAM. Go on. You do your depicting. Not a sad girl, or child-birth. Just depict Polly Dacey, hopping off. Hop!

He pushes Polly away and she goes off stage, leaving
Sam alone in the front of the stage with Miss Rosebush,
who has frozen again into her statue pose while Sam
becomes all naïve and wondering, almost stripped back to
his innocent self in the first act.

(*To audience.*) Don't look at me, London, all alone with my rose-bush, her with a posy on her nose and a stem black and shiny as a slug in the rain. Leave me be, Sewell Street, I'm all bare and private back in the country, happy as a gardener in this old heap of compost. I should have my gum-boots on! (*To Miss Rosebush.*) Can I pick you one by one?

MISS ROSEBUSH. I'll scratch you if you do.

Sam tries to pick a rose, and Miss Rosebush scratches him.

SAM. Ow! Rose bushes don't have nails.

MISS ROSEBUSH. It's a thorn.

SAM. No, you're a girl really.

MISS ROSEBUSH. I'm a rose in an evening dress. Can't you see?

SAM. You're a girl, and I want you.

He tries to kiss her, and only gets a mouthful of flowers.

I've heard of rosy cheeks, but this is ridiculous.

The string round Sam's arm gets tangled in the roses.

I've got some string to tie you up.

MISS ROSEBUSH. I'm not wilting. (*Pushes string away.*)

SAM. (*To audience.*) It's better than a flower show. Have a peek, Polly, I'm pie-eyed with petals. Look at me, Lucille, I'm fresh as a daisy, rolling in clover with a riot of roses. I want to bite off her lips and eat them like radishes. It'll be like going to bed with Kew Gardens. (*To Miss Rosebush.*) How do I get in?

Miss Rosebush turns round: a large sign on her back reads 'Keep Out'. She goes and arranges herself on the four-legged stool, so that one of her legs joins the others.

You've got more legs than a spider.

MISS ROSEBUSH. Don't you try and squash me.

Sam tries to pull the rose bush off Miss Rosebush's shoulders, but he fails, especially as his hands are still entangled in the string, which he cannot get off.

SAM. It's stuck tight as a lid on a honeypot. And I'm hot and buzzy as a bumble-bee. Can't I come in and tickle your petals? Where do you keep your pollen?

MISS ROSEBUSH. You might be a wasp. I don't know you.

SAM. I'm Sam Bennet, the Welsh poet. Perhaps you've heard of me.

MISS ROSEBUSH. Has anybody?

SAM. I've been too long in the hum-drumming humbug of a lackaday London. They're sensual falsifiers, over-familiars, mockers at make-believe. They live in an ever-Sunday weekday, with empty pews in their faces, preaching petty as a minister. They put drab on their young sons and corsets on their daughters.

But let's go, you and I, Miss Rosebush, for one short sunshaken summer, brief and vain as berries in our soon-lost love.

MISS ROSEBUSH. What a clever Celt's tongue you have in you . . . when you want to use it. It's like meadows in your mouth. Where will you take me?

SAM. To Laugharne, to Laugharne. Come to Laugharne over-steepled with briars, where you can grow and grow and grow, and no one to say no to you. It's a timeless, wild, Welsh, beguiling island of a town with seven public houses, a legendary lazy little black-magical bedlam by the sea.

MISS ROSEBUSH. Just you and me?

SAM. You and me and Mr Moon.

Miss Rosebush seems almost caught by the spell of words Sam has cast on her. Then she suddenly throws her rose-bush head back and laughs.

MISS ROSEBUSH. Sillybilly Bennet, falling for a bunch of flowers. I have *work* to do here. Roses and reputation only grow in London.

She rises and picks up a nearby megaphone as the crowd in the Exhibition drifts back into the room. All the time that she declaims her verses, Sam plucks at her and tries to tug her away.

SAM. To Laugharne . . . come on . . . I love you, rosy . . .

MISS ROSEBUSH. A cornucopia of phalluses
                 Cascade on the vermilion palaces
                 In arabesques and syrup rigadoons;
                 Quince-breasted Circes of the zenanas
                 Do catch this rain of cherry-winged
                     bananas
                 And saraband beneath the raspberry
                     moons.

Everyone howls and cheers. Sam tries to pull Miss Rose-bush away.

MISS ROSEBUSH. Will you get out of my limelight?

SAM. I just want to say I love you.

MISS ROSEBUSH. Scene-stealer.

SALVADOR. Who's that? He'll do anything for publicity.

GEORGE. He's a minor Welsh poet. Lemuel Bonnet, I think. No one would ever have heard of him if he hadn't dropped his own name so often.

MRS DACEY. That's not true. He'll be famous.

MISS ROSEBUSH. As a molester of virgins.

SAM. I love you. (*They walk forward.*)

MISS ROSEBUSH. You love my rose bush.

SAM. No. I love you. Do let me see you.

MISS ROSEBUSH. You wouldn't love me if I did.

SAM. I would.

MISS ROSEBUSH. Liar. You love somebody else.

SAM. I don't.

MISS ROSEBUSH. You love Lucille Harris. I know.

SAM. I don't love her.

MISS ROSEBUSH. Do you love me, then?

SAM. Yes, I do.

Miss Rosebush laughs and laughs and laughs.

MISS ROSEBUSH. You love my roses.

SALVADOR. (*Coming up with a giant pair of scissors.*) It's pruning time.

SAM. Come with me to Laugharne, and grow.

Salvador snaps the scissors in front of Sam's face. Sam cowers back.

SALVADOR. Don't grow too fast. (*To Miss Rosebush.*) Come and see your clippings.

MISS ROSEBUSH. I'd love to. (*They go off followed by the crowd.*)

MRS DACEY. They were so mean to you, my baby. You'll be greater than those porkers one day.

POLLY. You'll make us all famous. In the *News of the World*.

MR ALLINGHAM. Then perhaps someone will come along and buy some furniture. I knew it was a mistake to pull down the ceilings to get more in. Now the roof leaks, going to bed's like a shower-bath.

SAM. Miss Rosebush! (*Goes off, looking for her.*)

Mr Allingham begins handing the surrealist objects to Polly, who wheels them away in the pram. Gradually they begin to strip the whole exhibition.

MR ALLINGHAM. Still, there's always room for some more. Give us a hand, Polly.

POLLY. (*Putting the monster apple on the pram with the model.*) You'll never get it in.

MR ALLINGHAM. Plenty more room, plenty more room.

Polly wheels the apple off.

I may live with too much stuff, I admit it. But I need it all. It's good stuff and you can't have too much good stuff. You want all you can get of good stuff, pack it in and sit on it. This country's tight as a trivet, thank you nicely in its own patch of water, bursting with bric-à-brac, you couldn't squeeze an extra cat in. That's why we're so proud and private. Each of us lives in our own packed little island in our packed bigger island. And we don't want to give any of it away, certainly not to foreigners.

SAM. (*Coming back in and slouching listlessly.*) I want out, out to Aldebaran and back, sky-high and seascape, a life bigger and madder than an elephant with rabies.

Sam tries futilely to get the string off his arm.
Polly returns and loads up the pram with the fur jug and the stool with human legs.

Stop thief!

POLLY. I'm not a thief, silly. I'm a kidnapper. Look. (*Shows the four legs of the stool.*) Siamese twins!

She wheels off the last of the surrealist objects front-stage.

MR ALLINGHAM. You don't want out, Samuel. You're helpless in vast spaces, you've never even seen one. You're an aspidistra poet. Your howling heath's the pub on the corner. You couldn't even top a boiled egg when you first came to stay with us. Your mum had always done it for you.

SAM. So she had. Up with her knife and slice off the shell so I could get in. Like a womb with a view.

Sam looks at the surrealist 'Womb with a View' up the steps.

MR ALLINGHAM. Do you think we could get away with that too?

SAM. Ah, ah, at it again. What do you want more junk for? There won't be any room left for you soon. I'm getting out.

MR ALLINGHAM. Don't let me stop you. Came in for the night three years ago, and overstayed your welcome.

SAM. I'll really leave, then you'll be sorry. You don't want to let me go. You don't want to let anything go.

MR ALLINGHAM. (*Anguished.*) Adonis! He's the one I want. Never answers back when *he's* spoken to.

> *George appears on the steps and looks down aghast at the bare stage, where once there was a surrealist exhibition.*

GEORGE. You're not allowed to do that.

SAM. And you, George Ring, you're not allowed, full stop.

GEORGE. You put them back.

MR ALLINGHAM. We don't know where they've gone. Like Adonis.

GEORGE. I'll call for Salvador.

MR ALLINGHAM. That's right. Call for your new friends. Be loyal . . .

GEORGE. (*Softly.*) Stop thief!

MR ALLINGHAM. Go on, put us in prison. I knew it'd come to that. George Ring, copper's nark. Adonis!

> *He searches in every corner for Adonis.*

GEORGE. Donald!

> *Mr Allingham ignores him.*

(*To Sam.*) It's all your fault. There we were, all snug and set up till you moved in. We didn't even ask you. You just moved in and pushed me out.

SAM. I'm not staying any longer. I'm going. You can have your old Sewell Street. And your rotten poetry.

GEORGE. It's not rotten poetry. It's beautiful poetry. (*Declaims.*) 'O to be in England, now that April's here.'

> *Sam and George fence with poetry.*

SAM. Friend by enemy I call you out.

GEORGE. 'Hail to thee, blithe spirit,
    Bird thou never wert!'

SAM. You with a bad coin in your socket,
    You my friend there with a winning air.

GEORGE. 'Ill met by moonlight, proud Titania.'

SAM. I never thought to utter or think
My friends were enemies on stilts
With their heads in a cunning cloud.

GEORGE. ''Tis not too late to seek a newer world.'
Push off!

Mr Allingham points up to the 'Womb with a View'.

MR ALLINGHAM. Why don't you climb up there? Get back
where you belong?

*Sam pulls off the string at last and throws the clotted
mass at Mr Allingham. He is energetic again.*

SAM. All right, then, I'll use it as a pulpit. And when I've
finished I'll burst out again in a bloodybright Caesarean.

*He climbs up beside the 'Womb with a View', the
megaphone in his unentangled hand. The whole audience
at the exhibition gathers round, presuming another side-
show is about to start.*

GEORGE. (*Jealously.*) Get out, Sambo.

Salvador enters and stares aghast at the denuded stage.

SALVADOR. Where have they gone? (*To Sam.*) Would you
mind kindly stepping out of my creation?

SAM. But you're all *my* creation. Fig leaves of my imagination.
I wrote a play once about my version of Genesis. And, quite
frankly, it was full of ruddy genius. I called it 'Who Shot the
Emu?' Red and puce curtains, scarlet bananas on the ceiling. On
the floor, the skin of dead lepers.

GEORGE. How too fin-de-sièclical.

SAM. Knobs on nearly everything—except the doors, naturally.
I mean, there's nothing *useful* in creation. In each corner,
garrotted, an ancient herbalist. On the shelves, the whole works
of Edna St Vincent Millay. The book-ends are made of the left
arms of postmen. The curtain slowly rises. There is total darkness for three hours.

GEORGE. The audience, like all of Sam's audiences, is
tethered to their seats. With real ropes.

SAM. After three hours of total, absolute darkness, a voice:
'*Albert*, for crissake, put on the light!'

The audience laughs, to the fury of Salvador and George.

Sam puts the megaphone on the navel of the 'Womb with a View'.

I am the Original Umbilicus, ready to answer all your queries. Pop in a problem and I play a tune, even for the gentleman in the hysterical black moustache.

MRS DACEY. How should a young lady defend her honour?

SAM. There's only one way . . . Tin drawers.

Mr Allingham goes up the steps to examine the 'Womb with a View', the only object which might still conceal Adonis.

POLLY. And if he has a tin-opener?

SAM. Armour-plate.

MR ALLINGHAM. And if he has an armour-piercing howitzer? (*Peers through the window of the 'Womb with a View'.*)

SAM. Lie back and thank the Lord.

Mr Allingham begins to pull round the 'Womb with a View'. Adonis appears in a cage the other side of the womb.

MR ALLINGHAM. Adonis. My Adonis.

He struggles to free the statue out of the cage.

You wouldn't do it to a dog. And he's a Greek God.

SALVADOR. Leave my creation!

SAM. Here, Donald.

Mr Allingham tosses the statue down to Sam, where he stands in the middle of the bare stage. He runs with it through the surrealists and, just as he is trapped, he passes it on to Polly. A formal Rugby game develops with the Sewell Street set passing Adonis between them, avoiding the surrealists. The remainder of the crowd at the exhibition merely watches. Whistles blow: crowd sounds of the Welsh singing at the great Wales v. England games reverberate. An elaborate and lengthy Rugby dance takes place with Adonis, until Salvador at last gets it back, only to have George change sides, snatch it back and make off with it.

GEORGE. I'll help you, Donald!

*In the flickering lights, the crowd rushes off-stage, leaving
Sam alone there, and the crowd roaring for a touch-down.*

SAM. I want out. Out.

*By the 'Womb' Miss Rosebush appears. Sam reaches out
his arms to her.*

Miss Rosebush!

*Miss Rosebush goes off, and Sam stumbles forward in front
of the cut-out of the streets, which is wheeled in.*

INTERLUDE 4

*Sam is mooning and slouching about. The old tramp
with the pram and gramophone playing an old record, and
the policeman, pass by.*

SAM. I am a lonely nightwalker and a steady stander-at-
corners. I like to walk through the wet town after midnight,
when the streets are deserted and the window lights are nearly
out, gigantically sad on the damp steps, alone and alive by the
ghostly Embankment, while the trains go by, home and away, on
the glistening lines under the moon. And I never feel more a part
of the remote and overpressing world, I never feel more full of
love and arrogance and pity and humility, not for myself alone,
but for the living earth I suffer on and for the unfeeling systems
in the upper air, Mars and Venus and Lucille and Miss Rosebush,
bad, ragged women who'd pretend against the museum wall for a
cup of tea, the tramp scratching the disk of the dark, playing the
tunes that needle unrecorded time, while the law creeps back to
his kennel down the street.

I slouch in the crack of a derelict house, or wander terrified on
the empty stairs, or mooch in the bare bones of the bedrooms
while the miners in my village are going home singing their
songs with their arms around each other, or I gaze through the
smashed windows at the river or at nothing. And I look in the
stars for my Rose . . . showing a leg!

Sam pushes off the cut-out of the streets.

The scene is the over-stocked room in Sewell Street. It is more crammed than ever. The room is full of the objects from the Surrealist Exhibition, piled in every spare space. Even the 'Womb with a View' overhangs Polly's naked shoulders and the duck in the bath. Mrs Dacey, Mr Allingham and George are having tea. Adonis stands between Mr Allingham and George. Both fondle the statue lovingly from time to time.

A record of 'Sweet Summer Breeze' plays in the background as all sing and hum to it.

MRS DACEY.
MR ALLINGHAM.
GEORGE.   }(Sing.)
POLLY.

Sweet summer breeze,
Whispering trees,
Stars shining softly above,
Roses in bloom,
Wafting perfume
Sleep in a dreaming of love . . .

MRS DACEY. How many lumps?

MR ALLINGHAM. Always the same question. You've known me fifteen years, and you still don't know I always have three.

MRS DACEY. You could change your mind.

GEORGE. Donald wouldn't ever change his mind. It's an institution. Englishmen don't change their institutions. (*Pause.*) Nor their old chums.

MR ALLINGHAM. I was provoked.

MRS DACEY. (*Calling.*) Milk, Polly?

POLLY. Yes, Ma.

MRS DACEY. You must be freezing to death in there.

POLLY. Yes, Ma.

MRS DACEY. Well, why don't you get out?

POLLY. In a mo, Ma.

MRS DACEY. Is the water hot?

POLLY. I don't know. I'm having a dry bath.

MR ALLINGHAM. She's having a dry bath. I suppose you don't want to get your clothes wet.

POLLY. That's right. I'm getting out, if I *can*.

Polly looks angrily at the 'Womb with a View', then steps out of the bath. She is wearing all her clothes except her blouse, which she puts on. The duck, which bobs on the bath, sinks down.

MR ALLINGHAM. Why can't she take a wet bath like other people?

GEORGE. She's such a little jumbo, she wouldn't float.

MR ALLINGHAM. What's that got to do with having a bath?

GEORGE. You never know, do you? We found Sam drownded in the bath once. Only we got there too quick. We saved him.

There is a squiggling and crashing among the chairs. Rose appears, looking exactly the same as in her brief appearance three years back.

ROSE. You didn't ask me to have a cup of tea.

MRS DACEY. Well, we haven't seen you for three years.

ROSE. It's not polite not to ask someone who's staying with you to have a cup of tea.

Mrs Dacey gives Rose a cup of tea, after putting two lumps of sugar in it.

MR ALLINGHAM. (*Accusingly.*) You remembered how many lumps she had after three years.

MRS DACEY. I haven't had to think of it for so long that it's quite fresh in my mind.

POLLY. (*Joining them.*) Hallo, Rose. Nice to see you again. Has it been fun down there among the furniture?

ROSE. It's just like anywhere. Too many things with legs bothering you. (*Looks accusingly at the four-legged stool.*) And you still bring more in.

GEORGE. Why did you come to see us again, Rose, darling?

ROSE. It's dinner time, isn't it? Can't a girl have a cup of tea?

MRS DACEY. You've taken three years to find out you wanted one.

ROSE. I've been off tea.

MR ALLINGHAM. (*To George.*) There's still a space over

there. We should have brought the lamp-post too. I told you we could fit it in.

Sam enters. In his hands he is holding a huge bunch of roses, which is wet.

GEORGE. He's brought his garden in to see us. And the rain too.

MRS DACEY. Sam, I knew you'd remember. Mother's Day.

POLLY. That was six months ago. He brought them for me. Oh, Sam!

MR ALLINGHAM. No, I'm not going into the flower business. You won't change me. You can't grow roses from Chippendale.

SAM. I'll never live without roses again.

MRS DACEY. We'd better buy him a conservatory.

SAM. There she was, her head all roses, brighter than a seed packet.

GEORGE. Her with a rose on her nose.

SAM. I love her. One deepdrowning dawn, we'll fall down together in our red round rosy Newfoundland, in the pink-petalled roister of our love.

POLLY. Have a cup of tea, de . (*Sam shakes his head.*)

ROSE. A Bass, then?

Sam shakes his head again, and puts his roses in the gramophone horn, keeping one in his hand.

SAM. I want my rose bush.

MR ALLINGHAM. Who doesn't?

GEORGE. It's just like Maud. Lord Alfred Tennyson's Maud. You remember. 'I said to the rose, "The brief night goes In babble and revel and wine . . ."'

SAM. '"O young lord-lover, what sighs are those, For one that will never be thine?"'

GEORGE & SAM. '"But mine, but mine," so I sware to the rose, "For ever and ever, mine."'

Sam throws George his single rose.

GEORGE. That's beautiful. You are a clever little Sambo, when you're taken down a peg.

POLLY. Who's this you love now?

SAM. Her body's black and curious as a roadmender's hole and her head's the biggest bloody bouquet you ever saw.

MRS DACEY. Not the girl you saw at the exhibition?

SAM. Yes. And I won't ever see her again. I've come to pack my bags and go. I'll live alone, if I can't have my rose bush.

All begin to titter and laugh.

GEORGE. What about Lucille? Don't you love your little Lucille?

SAM. We're bored with each other. I love Miss Rosebush.

MR ALLINGHAM. Won't she be just as boring?

SAM. Never. She's all fire and budding and soft sweet smell.

MRS DACEY. What a romantic baby! He'll never learn, will he? Off with those wet trews.

MR ALLINGHAM. Never.

POLLY. Never.

Sam pushes off Mrs Dacey as she tries to take off his trousers.

GEORGE. Never.

ROSE. Never.

SAM. You mean old kill-loves. You want everything to be dull as chapels. Like you are. I want my rose. And I'll never see her again.

MRS DACEY. Perhaps she'll come to have a cup of tea.

SAM. She won't. (*Sits on the trampoline.*)

MR ALLINGHAM. She drinks tea just like other people.

SAM. She doesn't. She drinks milk and honey.

MRS DACEY. Milk and no sugar. You'll see.

SAM. (*Buries his face in his hands.*) Let me be.

Rose bends over the trampoline above Sam.

GEORGE. Here's Rose to see you.

SAM. (*Looking up.*) You're a maggot.

ROSE. (*Falling on Sam like a bird of prey.*) Like hell I am. All girls are the same. You'll find out.

SAM. Never. Let me go.

As Sam struggles unsuccessfully to shove Rose off him, there is the sound of scrambling and Miss Rosebush clambers in.

ALL. It's Miss Rosebush, to see Sam Bennet.

SAM. Don't tease.

ALL. It is. It is.

MISS ROSEBUSH. Sam. Sam Bennet.

SAM. (*Looking up.*) You!

MISS ROSEBUSH. Me.

SAM. How did you get here?

MISS ROSEBUSH. I wanted a cup of tea.

> *All laugh. Mrs Dacey pours her a cup of tea as Sam conducts Miss Rosebush to the tea-things.*

SAM. You want milk and honey.

MRS DACEY. Milk and no sugar.

MISS ROSEBUSH. That's right. Milk and no sugar.

> *She drinks by just putting a rose from her head in the teacup.*

SAM. You've come to see me.

MISS ROSEBUSH. I've come to have some tea.

SAM. Take off your roses.

MISS ROSEBUSH. I don't pluck in public.

SAM. My suitcase is still packed in the basin. And the duck's sunk in the bath. I want out. Out to Laugharne with you. Now.

MR ALLINGHAM. Isn't London good enough for you?

SAM. No, it's all soot and funeral families and graceless anonymous people lively as wet brollies. It's death to roses and all the proud gardeners.

MR ALLINGHAM. Sam, Sam, if you take away . . . Miss Rosebush (*all titter*) you'll make something happen. And I thought you only wanted things to happen to you. Or you wouldn't have come here in the first place.

SAM. I wish I never had. I can stand on my own. It's a trap here, to smother me and flay me alive.

MRS DACEY. (*Fondling him.*) Poor little bunny.

SAM. (*To Miss Rosebush.*) Come with me. Out of here. We'll go down together, one cool body weighted with a boiling stone, on to the falling, blank white, entirely empty sea, and never rise.

MISS ROSEBUSH. Oh, Sam, Sam, what would you do with me? How would you live with me?

SAM. I'd turn lines for gold, coin verses for overdrafts, and we'd live on a holiday mint of shillings for nothing, owe nobody nuppence, all proud and only us.

MISS ROSEBUSH. What'll you do, when you're so rich?

GEORGE. (*Sings.*) Said the bells of Shoreditch.

SAM. When I am a rich man with my own bicycle and can have beer for breakfast, I shall give up writing poetry altogether and just be absolutely disgusting.

MISS ROSEBUSH. Count me out.

SAM. No, you're in.

MISS ROSEBUSH. It takes two to make a couple.

SAM. A couple can be one.

POLLY. Couples become families, little happy families. There's always a family wherever Sam goes.

SAM. I'll walk alone with my love in the warm, spinning middle, where no intruding strangers can poke their nosy parkers. I don't need friends in my own rose-garden.

GEORGE. Little Sam Ungrateful. I knew he would be.

POLLY. Forgetting Pretty Polly.

MRS DACEY. And Mrs Mother Dacey.

MR ALLINGHAM. And Mr Daddy Allingham.

ROSE. And Rosie under the sofa.

GEORGE. And what about poor Lucille?

SAM. She's nothing to me now.

ROSE. Gave up her youth to you, her honour, her income.

POLLY. Kept you, and cared for you.

MRS DACEY. Bought you galoshes in winter.

MR ALLINGHAM. Put keys on ice in case you had nose-bleeds.

ALL. Poor Lucille. Poor Lucille. (*They pretend to weep.*)

SAM. She won't miss me.

ALL. She will.

SAM. I don't care. I'm taking Miss Rosebush to Laugharne.

MISS ROSEBUSH. Are you sure you want me?

SAM. Yes. For ever. (*All laugh mockingly.*)

MISS ROSEBUSH. Don't you want to see me?

SAM. Yes. Yes.

MISS ROSEBUSH. You won't want me then.

SAM. I will. I will.

The girl takes off her rose bush and reveals herself to be
LUCILLE. *All laugh mockingly.*

SAM. No.

LUCILLE. Yes.

GEORGE. You want her for ever. (*Laughs.*)

POLLY. You'll never leave her. (*Laughs.*)

MRS DACEY. You'll always love her. (*Laughs.*)

MR ALLINGHAM. It's all the same, Sam, wherever you go. It's all the same.

ROSE. I told you, girls are all alike. You can't escape it.

SAM. No.

GEORGE. Come back to your family.

POLLY. In Cardiff or Paddington.

LUCILLE. Come back to your lovely.

ROSE. It's all the same everywhere.

MRS DACEY. Every woman is your mother.

MR ALLINGHAM. Every man your father.

LUCILLE. Every popsy a Lucy.

GEORGE. And all of us your selves.

ROSE. And a rose is a rose is a rose is just a bloody rose.

They all pluck at Sam with picking fingers, holding him back among them.

SAM. (*Backing away.*) I want out. Back to Wales now. Where's my case? I'm off to Paddington. Catch the first train out.

All the Sewell Street set surround Sam. They catch him towards them, saying their lines with faster and faster rhythm, until they sound like a train gathering speed, and real train noises sound off-stage.

MR ALLINGHAM. You can't ever leave us.

MRS DACEY. You can't live alone now.

POLLY. Who'll do your cooking?

LUCILLE. Your mending, your darning?

ROSE. Helpless as a baby.

GEORGE. Little Baby Sambo.

ALL. Never grow up.

MR ALLINGHAM. Stay with your old friends.

MRS DACEY. People who know you.

POLLY. We'll look after you.

LUCILLE. You know you can trust us.

ROSE. For ever and ever.

GEORGE. Little baby Sambo.

ALL. Never grow up.

SAM. (*Shouting.*) Out . . . out . . . out.

The Sewell Street set each produce a bottle or glass or long cigar out of a chair or a pocket. They jab them into Sam's face as their train rhythm gets faster and faster.

MR ALLINGHAM. Have a Bass.

MRS DACEY. Have a glass.

POLLY. Have a fag.

LUCILLE. Have a drag.

ROSE. Have a tot.

GEORGE. Nice and hot.

ALL. Never grow up.

All repeat their lines faster and faster, until the rhythm of the train is loud. They hunt Sam through the room and up the stairs, where he bars their way in front of the bath with a chair so they cannot pursue him. They fall back, baffled, still making their rhythm, until they draw back through the furniture and the rhythm dies into the distance.

SAM. No. I'll find the roses, the lonely roses. In my mind, I'll make a garden of gaudy. You can skulk there in the sin-stripping, seven skin-stripping city, you strangers with social knives all alive for gutting poets. You can flay your bright boily boys in from the provinces. You can chuck them to the drink dogs and gas them with fag-ends. You can sap them like a maple so the poetry runs mouldy. You can spike the clock so the years lag by, and nothing's doing and nothing's done in the hourless hours. You can mincemeat our livers and put out our lights . . .

The stage has darkened until there is only one spot left on Sam. There is total quiet.

But there's an eighth skin inside my skull. You'll never get in there. My eyes turn inwards. I turn in on myself. In my skull is my house. It keeps the world and the weather out. There I make my own weathering world inside, all sea and sky in a brain's bare room.

Behind Sam, the chant of the Sewell Street set begins to rise. The lights go up. Mr Allingham and Mrs Dacey stand

*above him, bottle and glass held downwards like daggers
now. The other four creep around him, their bottles and
cigars held ready to pierce like stilettos. Sam is forced
to the middle of the stairs, shouting above the chant.*

Mr Christ, is there no answer for a sociable poet? Must he live
off people who can't leave him alone? No answer. There never is.
Just the sad cycle . . .

*Mr Allingham stabs Sam with the bottle. Sam sinks back
on the mattresses where he has been laid after drowning
in the bath in the first act.*

Of sin and Sunday, moral as a plague . . .

Mrs Dacey stabs Sam with her glass.

Till you're done . . .

Polly stabs Sam with her cigar.

And you haven't done it . . .

Lucille stabs Sam with her cigar.

The tenth of what you want to do . . .

Rose stabs Sam with her bottle.

Before you're black dead . . . and done.

*George stabs Sam with his bottle. Sam goes into a great
fit of coughing into his hand and looks at the result.*

Blood . . . that's the stuff.

*Sam lies back on the mattresses, apparently dead.
Polly begins to cry over Sam's body in exactly the same
way as she has depicted in the third scene.*

POLLY. I'm a tragedienne. I'm crying because my lover's dead.
His name was Sam and he had green eyes and yellow hair. He was
ever so short. Darling, darling, darling Sam. He's dead.

*All the Sewell Street set laugh at Polly's depicting, and
she suddenly stops crying and smiles.*

I was only depicting. I can do being glad, too.

*All except Sam line up in procession, bearing their
bottles and glasses and cigarettes like funeral objects
before them. They chant happily as a requiem on their
way out, to organ music.*

MR ALLINGHAM. Have a Bass.

MRS DACEY. Have a glass.

POLLY. Have a fag.

LUCILLE. Have a drag.

ROSE. Have a tot.

GEORGE. Nice and hot.

ALL. Never grow up.

Until you're done . . .

The requiem fades away. Once the stage is quiet, Sam
rises from the mattresses and walks front-stage. He has
his suitcase in his hand. Over a loudspeaker, a voice:

VOICE. The Cardiff train now standing at Platform Number
One will leave in one minute.

SAM. Twenty-four years remind the tears of my eyes.

(Bury the dead for fear that they walk to the grave in
labour.)

In the groin of the natural doorway I crouched like a
tailor.

Sewing a shroud for a journey

By the light of the meat-eating sun.

Dressed to die, the sensual strut begun,

With my red veins full of money,

In the final direction of the elementary town

I advance for as long as forever is.

A NOTE ON THE LONDON PRODUCTION

by JAMES ROOSE-EVANS

IN THE summer of 1965 Allan Davis sent me the script of a play saying, 'I think this is more your kind of play than mine.' Thus it was that I came to read Andrew Sinclair's play based upon the unfinished novel of Dylan Thomas. The play is not great literature, indeed Thomas himself assessed it as 'a mixture of Oliver Twist, Little Dorrit, Kafka, Beachcomber and good old three-adjectives-a penny, belly-churning Thomas, the Rimbaud of Cwmdonkin Drive', but I knew that it would work as *entertainment*, as a piece of theatre. The invention, the business, the effects of that first production have now become part of the final text.

Once committed to a production there were two main problems to solve: the casting of the central role of Sam Bennet and the physical staging of the play. I auditioned a young film actor who had already made an impressive stage début at the Royal Court in a play called *Skyvers*. At his audition for me David Hemmings read from the play, sang, danced, performed conjuring tricks, improvised, and seemed so perfectly right for the part that there was never any question in my mind. Bursting with talent—he is also a skilful caricaturist—completely uninhibited, reckless even, with a superb sense of comedy timing, and uncannily like the nineteen-year-old Dylan in temperament and behaviour, he seemed to me one of those exciting gambles. Rehearsals were often a nightmare as he collapsed from nervous prostration, caught a cold, lost his voice—a compulsive talker and story-teller, he had to be ordered home after rehearsal!—or drove with abandoned impetuosity. The whole play and production rested on his shoulders with a part that demands considerable technical virtuosity and vocal range, but we all knew that he was so superbly right, so responsive to direction, fertile in invention and so outgoing as a person, that we all would have marched to Wales and back for him had it been necessary!

While the rest of the casting proceeded I had initial sessions with Michael Young, one of the most versatile of our younger designers. At first we experimented with the possibility of using a central revolve and two towers, one on each side of the stage, but in the model this proved to be cumbersome, cramped and old-fashioned. Something freer, more inventive, was required. But what? The opening scene of the play and the interludes I had already cleared out of the way by proposing to have these filmed, but there remained still the buffet at Paddington station, Mr Allingham's overstocked house, a bathroom, the Gayspot night-club, the Surrealist Exhibition of 1936 and a return to Mr Allingham's house for the final scene. Michael Young's eventual solution was as brilliant as it was simple.

On the principle of the Elizabethan stage he designed an upper and lower gallery which extended the whole thirty-one-foot width of the stage, with exits, upstairs and down, in the extreme left- and right-hand corners. All that the audience saw on entering the theatre was a long brick wall across the back of the stage, six feet in height, and above it a long platform like a narrow shelf set back from which was another brick wall, also six feet in height. A portable wooden staircase led from one level to another. In the centre of the stage stood a large, trucked white screen, ready for the first filmed sequence—after which a pulley screen was lowered from the roof for the remaining filmed inter-ludes. It was all very bare, austere and, deliberately, uninviting. When, after the opening film sequence, the lights came up for the station scene, the screen was trucked around to reveal the back of the buffet—large Victorian mirror and shelves—while the counter, a separate trucked unit, supporting a heavy old-fashioned tea urn, was rolled into place. The tables and chairs had been pre-set behind the screen. Upstairs, a large screen unrolled bearing a reproduction of the glass roof of Paddington station. The staircase on stage left became one of the staircases at Paddington leading from the upper platforms to the lower.

For Mr Allingham's house the tables and chairs remained on stage, as also did an old pram with a horn gramophone which was used as part of the action in the Paddington scene. The station buffet wall and counter were pushed to one side where, like the tables, chairs and pram, they became part of the junk in Mr Allingham's. Downstairs, the wall opened in the middle in the form of two six-foot-wide doors rolling on castors and each covered with a montage of furniture. From the central alcove thus revealed disgorged all the remaining furniture, while the portable ladder was moved to centre stage, and similarly on the upper platform the back wall had opened up to reveal the bathroom in the upstairs alcove. Behind these two upstairs doors were sliding panels on tracks to provide a glossy entrance for Lucille in the night-club scene, while behind these yet again were two further panels, white in colour, ready to frame 'The Womb-With-A-View', the central object at the Surrealist Exhibition, which was trucked forward from the back of the alcove, being covered with blankets for the Allingham scenes so that it resembled a large mound of bedding. Cat ladders on both sides and at the back enabled the actors, unseen by the audience, to climb up or down from one area to another.

Downstairs, for the surrealist scene, the brick wall proved to have other hinged flaps which, when opened and folded across, revealed an enormous pair of crimson lips on a white background, spanning the stage, while from under the alcove the various surrealist objects on stands were carried forward and set in place by the actors.

For the Gayspot all the furniture was restored to its place under the platform, the doors closed up, the ladder moved to stage right, so that customers entered, as it were, from the pavement above, coming down into the night-club, while the wall upstairs was picked out in hundreds of tiny bulbs spelling the word 'Gayspot'. In the centre of the stage was a circular staircase, which in the previous scene had been trucked forward on its side, covered with mattresses. To one side was a piano and microphone, while at the far end was the buffet mirror with the bar counter turned around, revealing on its other side a different shape, style and pattern. The tables and chairs remained.

It sounds and was basically a simple solution to the problems of staging the play, and was only complicated in that it called for considerable patience, routine and practice on the part of the actors (most of whom were already playing several roles), who had to set and strike the stage each time in a minimum of light, under very cramped conditions. Striking was even more important than setting, since everything had to be put back in pre-arranged positions under the back platform in order to avoid chaos building up in the semi-darkness.

Of the filmed interludes certain critics remarked, 'Surely the talkies had come in by 1936!' thereby revealing their complete ignorance of costs, especially of filming. By shooting on 16 m.m. and avoiding dubbing (a lengthy and expensive process), and employing a non-union camera man who accepted a token fee, the entire film, including hire of projector for five weeks, cost only £170, where a talkie, involving union rates, would have cost about £1,500—half the entire production costs!

More important, however, was the intention behind the filming. To have made a conventional movie would have been totally alien to the production. After all, we were not trying to make either a film or even a thirties-style film. Since it was impossible, scenically, to have Sam Bennet smash an entire set of Victorian china at every performance, as the text requires— apart from the possible use of shadow play—film became the only other solution, and once you use film in a production then theatrically, stylistically, such a device must be carried through the production. It was thus that I solved the problem of the scene changes. My idea was to show Sam's nineteen-year-old fantasy of himself smashing up the home thrown up on the screen of his adolescent imagination, and then to contrast this with the reality of Sam himself first seen at Paddington station, dwarfed by the immensity of London. The choice of Keystone Cops style for the opening film sequence, which was Andrew Sinclair's idea, was a deliberate Dylanesque joke and as such enjoyed by the audience.

In the second half of the production in which film was used only once (one must never flog a stylistic device but use it sparingly) we attempted to show, by a more sophisticated style of filming and by having a recorded voice on tape, the develop- ment of Sam's tastes and fantasies, less flamboyantly adolescent.

It is all a question of style. The play itself is not a serious, psychological, analytical study of the man, Dylan Thomas—as some critics would have it—nor does it attempt to be an academic reproduction of the thirties. It is a timeless fantasy of any young artist up from the provinces for the first time, journeying through the inferno of London—the Adventures of Sam Bennet: a picaresque novel in the tradition of Fielding, with all the broad caricature and adolescent vitality of Dickens. It is a kaleidoscopic burst of fireworks in the mind of an adolescent, and only intermittently autobiographical. The production, with its swiftly changing sets, like a series of coloured handkerchiefs and white rabbits endlessly appearing from the magician's hat; by its use of film, songs, music and overall *sense of fun*, must attempt to match this. If it is not fun, it fails. If the audience comes out moved, refreshed and chuckling, then it has succeeded.

During the first Allingham scene Sam asks if he can ring up Lucille, and George hands him a telephone that has an unattached lead. Sam does not notice this, and George, hidden by the mound of mattresses, speaks into the horn of the old gramophone (which goes on playing 'All Alone By The Telephone') pretending to be Lucille. When the conversation was ended I had George unclip the horn, and from this moment in the scene it became an extension, first of George, then of Sam. I have always been intrigued by the ease with which the imagination can convert a simple object into whatever we wish it to represent. Children do this all the time, and in the theatre it has very ancient traditions. Even today, in the Kathakali dance drama of India, if an actor kneels down in front of a simple wooden bench he is praying at the altar of his gods; if he lies down on it and places his head on his hands he has gone to bed; if he walks gingerly across it then he is traversing a steep ravine; he crouches down behind it, rises up, steps on to it and, shading his eyes, looks to the distant horizon, then he has climbed a high mountain; if he turns it upside-down and sits in it then he is paddling a canoe down the rapids; if he upends it and scrambles up it then he has climbed a tree. It is the basic principle of 'On your imaginary forces work!' It is the essence of poetry. Playing with objects, playing with words and images, was a device that Dylan Thomas used repeatedly, often with great effect.

Thus, in this scene, I suggested to Doug Fisher, who was playing George Ring, that he use the horn in varying ways: clasped phallically between his thighs, the large tulip end outwards as he swung from the roof and declaimed: 'I'm going to buy a hammock, then I'll go to bed like a sailor!'; or, sprawling seductively across the mattresses, as a telescope with which to look at Sam, like Nelson taking his first peep at Lady Hamilton; or, balancing the narrow funnel on the floor, perching on it as in a chair or on a chamber pot; blaring into it like a barker at a fairground with a megaphone: 'Harum-scarum, be bold and bare 'em!'; or, holding it to Sam's ear and speaking very softly, purring: 'Didn't you really have any idea where to stay?'; then, as Sam and he recite poetry, they both develop the game, Sam wearing it on his head like a coolie hat, or both pretending to be old men and the one shouting into it as the other holds it to his ear like an ear-trumpet. Not only does the horn become a visual joke in a Dylanesque manner, but one sees Sam intrigued by George and the two discovering and sharing a common vein of fantasy that draws them together.

To look back on the whole experience of *Skin Trade* is to look back on an atmosphere of gaiety and intense excitement, so that even the hazards of absenteeism and other crises were caught on the wing. The final week, as always for a director, was one of considerable strain, as one martialled together the component parts—lighting, sound, film, scene changes, effects, business—fusing them into a whole. Almost always at this stage that unity of performance that has been achieved in rehearsal disintegrates as the actors take time to relate to and integrate with new factors. During this period the director concentrates less on the finer points of acting or interpretation than on the hundred and one technical points: the positioning of a lamp, a late lighting cue, or a too-quick fade, a music cue too loud, or too soon, a piece of furniture wrongly set, someone's make-up to be toned down, a prop missing, a wrong detail of costume or someone can't do their quick-change in time (right, let's do it several times!), a wig that has to be re-dressed, a corner of the set that has a light leak and must be canvassed, a note to actors not to bang the dressing-room doors, and not to talk during performance, a blue bulb to be rigged for the prompt, or the projector breaks down and a specialist has to be brought in, the taped-over voice still not coinciding with the images in the final film sequence, and so on. A special technical rehearsal has to be called with Robert Eddison to perfect the fall of the materials over his umbrella: they fall either to the left or to the right or in front or behind, but not on top! On the opening night they fall on top of the umbrella, but the black material (that has supported them under the roof until released) hangs down from the roof completely obscuring for one-half of the audience the upper stage, where the bathroom scene is about to take place. I race around and get two actors to go on stage, once the lights have faded on the lower stage at the commencement of the bathroom scene, one riding on the shoulders of the other, to jerk down the material and so save the situation. Neither actor objected or said we'd feel such fools. They just went on and did it, and so absorbed were Bridget Turner and David Hemmings that neither noticed this double-bodied apparition stretching up thirteen feet and jerking down the material in front of them.

A great deal of improvisation was employed during rehearsals. The more an actor extends into improvisation and imagines other scenes from the life of his character, the more rounded is his characterization and the more adaptable is he to any mishap or accident in performance. Thus, when one night Sam's bottle fell off as he was undressing to get into the bath I gasped and thought, Now what happens to the plot and the resulting comedy? Two or three speeches later, Bridget Turner as Polly—a brilliant virtuoso performance this—before giving Sam his drink of eau-de-Cologne, picked up the bottle, put it firmly back on his finger, saying: 'You've got to have this on, you know. You can't have your drink without your bottle on!' Whereupon David Hemmings improvised to the effect that he had only just got the bottle *off* and now she had gone and put it back on again! In the following scene, as Mr Allingham brought him downstairs, he went on about having got the bottle off, and so closely and spontaneously was all this woven into the text and the performance that there was never a hint to an outsider that anything was unscripted. Of course all actors will adapt to an emergency, but there are not many who can so easily catch a moment on the wing like this and *use it creatively*, weaving it into the fabric of the play. Jacques Copeau used to speak of the Compagnie des Quinze as a company of artists, of 'actor-creators', and it is this intense creative participation in the work of rehearsals, opening up the play, freeing the text, that leads to that joyousness and authority that must have distinguished the Commedia dell' Arte at its peak.

HAMPSTEAD, 1966.